ENCHANTING THE FAE PRINCE

Kingdoms of Lore Book Two

ALISHA KLAPHEKE

PROLOGUE

In the thick and starlit wood, the witch with hair as green as ivy worked at her magic loom.

A castle—built by long-forgotten ancients and instilled with powers of its own—protected her from the forest's nightly fog and howling scar wolves. For she was not an ordinary magic-worker, such as a water mage or another breed of witch. Her life's tale held no frog princes or bubbling cauldrons, unless you counted the one used for supper. The witch of the Forest of Illumahrah had but one power.

She was the Matchweaver.

Inside the sprawling castle's aged stone walls, the Mageloom—a rainbow of wool—spanned the entirety of the great hall. The loom's magic-infused frame was the same dark color as the rough-hewn timbers in the pitched ceiling. Muttering spells as she slid the shuttle, the witch threaded sunrise pink into ocean blue and deep forest green behind sparkling plum.

A vision in the weaving halted her moving hands.

She cocked her head and studied the image that only she, the fifth Matchweaver in history, could see. A face.

"Hmm."

Leaning back in her creaking willow-branch chair, she took up her pipe and blew a nice ring. A smile like a painter's stroke stretched her parchment cheeks. Finally.

"You are mine to match, fae knight, son to the Lady of the Agate Palace, the Queen of the Hill. I will match you well."

The castle's foundation vibrated as if horses galloped close by, and the witch's smile grew. Beside the north window, dust fell from a sconce, but the vibrations weren't overwhelming. They didn't knock the stag tapestry from the wall or bother the women who worked on the castle grounds.

Only the witch felt the drum in her toes, the flagstone floor purring underfoot like a cat. She'd been a great witch before the castle had called her to this position. Her power had doubled—perhaps tripled, if she measured it on a sunny day—since taking this role so very, very long ago.

Crafted for the Matchweaver, the castle's magic lived inside the stone walls. As legend had it, three powerful ancients had sacrificed themselves to be buried beneath the foundation, all in the name of love, all for the good of the kingdom of Lore. Their inborn magic suffused the place—a shimmering, diaphanous cloud hovering over the grounds, much like the fog in the wood. Every day, that power soaked into the witch, changed her blood, and pulled the Sight from her soul all the way to her eyes so she could read the Mageloom.

Now, the loom's image shifted and began to fade. Only the broad shoulders and one side of the fae's chiseled jaw remained. The witch knew him and not only because of his pointed ears and otherworldly eyes. He visited now and again. Some claimed he did so to keep an eye on the witch. They said he loved the terrible princess of Lore like a cousin. But maybe he longed for power like his mother and like so many fae. The magic buried here drew such folk. She'd find them just beyond her boundary, staring with glittering, hungry eyes at the castle though they themselves didn't know the reason for their longing.

"I will see a rich princess as your match, Prince Werian," she said around the stem of her pipe, "or perhaps a noble lady in need of some adventure. She will have fine blood. High blood. She will be worthy of you."

Of course, the fae in the weaving could not hear a word of the witch's lofty and ambitious ramblings, but that didn't matter to the witch. She was her own best company.

For now.

"Soon, I will see your match in my loom. Your mother will praise my work and reward me with a place at your hearth, among the beautiful fae. I will finally escape this world of low humans, most of whom aren't worth the wool I use to match them."

And with that, she went to bed. Her dreams showed her the Agate Court, the home of the Queen in the Hill. A court with walls of moon-white fae birch, spinning dancers dressed in rubies, and on every table—bowls and bowls of spirit agate, found only in the fae's realm.

She'd managed to wager a large piece off a lesser fae three decades back, and though the shimmering black agate was long gone, soaked fully into her being, she recalled with perfect detail the feeling of it breathing life into her. The stones suffused fae and witches with energy that sang through their blood and flesh, enhancing their inborn powers. Sighing, the witch rubbed her fingers together, remembering the tingling feel of the stone as it had fed her.

With such stores of magical agate, such massive amounts of power at hand, the fae could keep the witch alive forever. She might possibly, in fact, grow younger and find herself a fine fae knight.

CHAPTER 1

RHIANNE

Love was worth the risk. Wasn't it?

Rhianne stared at the starlit wood, a nervous tingle in her feet. Around her, the villagers sang second-harvest songs and danced in haphazard circles near the crackling bonfire, drunk on ale and the excitement of the autumnal equinox. The townsfolk were oblivious to the conflict raging inside her, however. Go or stay? What was the practical choice here?

"Look at that left-handed goat, thinking of heading for the enchanted wood," Odo the brewer whispered beyond the nearest of the bonfires.

She would not turn around and look at the man she had refused to work for, the brewer with the temper of a wet cat on a good day and that of a fevered bull on a bad.

Harold the blacksmith, made a noise of agreement. As the cobbler's niece, Rhianne had made him three pairs of shoes. Very wealthy, he was. "I hope she goes in and never comes out," the blacksmith said. "I don't like how my daughter looks up to her. Just because someone is good with shoes doesn't mean they're right in the head."

The insults pierced Rhianne like arrowheads, but she held her ground and refused to show the pain to them. She'd had plenty of practice. But maybe tonight would change it all...

It was Mabon, the one night of the year when maidens from the western province of the kingdom could seek the Matchweaver, who lived in an enchanted castle in the wood. A witch by birth, the Matchweaver was chosen by the castle and given the power to see a maiden's love match in the magical Mageloom. The northern province went to the witch at Lughnasadh, the Easterners visited on Beltane, and the southern dwellers at Imbolc. Without the witch, none could find their matches, their love, their partners for life.

With a deep breath, Rhianne set her ale on the ground and faced the towering oaks in the distance. Nine girls, younger than Rhianne by at least four years, had left earlier in the night, making their own routes toward the witch, hoping to hear a prophecy about whom they should wed in the coming year.

Rhianne knew well she should've walked into the woods already if she was going to do it. The fog, filled with legendary dangers and wolves alike, would be rising soon. It was nearly too late to leave at all.

A particularly raucous, boot-stomping song concluded. Couples embraced. Families teased one another as several boys lined up to jump the bonfire for luck.

Swallowing against the lump in her throat, Rhianne fisted her naked fingers, fingers devoid of wedding rings or copper mother bands. An invisible rope cinched her heart. Not even her one remaining family member—Uncle Cane—was here to ease her loneliness. He rarely strayed from home these days. She raised her eyes to the forest and began to walk, the stubbled fields crunching under her well-worn shoes and the stars winking above.

Behind her, the shouts of encouragement given to the lads jumping the fire faded, as did the singing.

Her ankle rolled, but she straightened and kept on.

Grabbing her skirts to keep the hem from dragging, she stepped over a rotting oak and picked up an animal path.

"The witch will turn you away, Cobbler!" The blacksmith called out, his voice like a raven's caw.

The wheelwright chuckled loudly at the potential horror of the witch keeping Rhianne's match locked in secret forever. "If she is lucky. If not, the Matchweaver will twist her into some foul creature a man could never love."

"Maybe she'll transform her into a snake." Odo's voice cut through the increasing fog. "She certainly has the mind of one."

Rhianne flicked the fingers of one hand over her shoulder at Odo before disappearing under the moon shadows cast by the towering trees.

"Oh ho!" The entire crowd guffawed at her insulting gesture.

They could all go hang.

She didn't bother fighting the nervous smile tugging at her lips. She was headed for the Matchweaver's castle. Here was a possibility. A chance at finding someone to take her side.

Though she'd been a mature woman for a few years,

this was her first time visiting the witch, as all maidens longing for love did at the equinox. She hadn't avoided this trip into the starlit forest because so many thought she was unlovable or because she was uninterested in the witch's prophecies. The war had interrupted all village traditions. Not once in her lifetime, but twice now.

But finally, life had resumed its rhythms, and so here she was, stepping over last year's fallen leaves and around the thicket of musky-scented brazenberries toward the depths of the woods and its witch.

The king had banished the witch to her estate, making it so that she could only leave at the permission and pleasure of the royal family. The king's actions had shocked Rhianne. The witch was quite nearly a goddess to the people. Granted, the witch had risen up against the princess, but if the king had listened to the witch from the start, none of it would've happened—the lovely Princess Aurora wouldn't have had all that horrible trouble. Rhianne wouldn't be ignoring the Matchweaver, that was certain.

The married women in town had described the enchanted castle in the wood, and Rhianne walked more quickly, wanting to see if the images she'd drawn in her mind's eye were accurate. She'd heard of a curtain wall of blackened stone surrounding a courtyard. Inside, gardens of yarrow, hyssop, nettle, and calendula grew as tall as the portcullis at the gate.

There had been talk of the women who lived with the witch, the ones who chose not to wed their matches, who instead made a life in the wood. The women supposedly tended the animals and picked the herbs the witch used from day to day. At night, the women slept in one of the outbuildings, all lined up on cots in the same room, like sisters. It shocked her that they could live there with that frightening woman after all she'd done.

What if she made such a choice? What if she never even had the chance to choose that option? The witch could turn her away, as the villagers teased. What would she do if the witch refused her? Rumor held that the witch sometimes barred maidens from the keep where the loom sat in its legendary chamber of colored glass and spelled walls. If the witch attempted to change Rhianne's form into a lowly beast or slithering reptile for some accidental slight, there was little she could do about it. She may as well shuck her trepidation and simply do her best to be courageous.

A shuffling sounded to her right. Scar wolves—named for the huge, black markings that crossed their massive heads—made their home in this wood. She respected their claim to the land, and they weren't conditioned to be as bloodthirsty as those trained by the enemy country of Wylfen, but still, she had no desire to meet with such a beast in the dark. She halted, her heart surging.

Two deer, pelts glistening with the evening's chill moisture, leapt over the game trail she followed and dashed into a stand of paper birches.

Chiding herself for startling so easily, she focused on the softly glowing mushrooms that lined the gleaming, starlit path. She'd always been good at sensing direction during hunts, and she knew well the witch's magic-infused abode was due east. Though Rhianne was not a true huntress, she had in fact taken down many hares and one impressively sized doe with her bow and arrows during the war. Before and after that, she had crafted shoes for the army, a necessary duty to keep the soldiers' and knights' feet from developing debilitating diseases. It was not a glorious task, making shoes. But it was nothing to be ashamed of either.

Regardless, her nightly dreams placed her on a dappled gray charger, bow in hand and wrath in her eyes. But the rest of those recurring dreams...

She laughed quietly at herself. In them, she saw a man beside her, a stranger astride a pure white stallion, wielding a sword that glittered like a woodbeetle's back.

No, that was fantasy. She jumped a bubbling creek and waded through waist-high ferns, setting her mind to reason. She would be pleased with a fine man from a neighboring town who could use her cobbler skills at his workshop or perhaps support her own small industry in a new place, away from those who loved to tease her. Away from horrible Odo Brewer. She didn't even wish for love. She only needed support, a partner. Of course, if he were handsome, she wouldn't mind. As long as he wasn't the kind of handsome that Odo boasted. Good looks combined with a savage heart.

Like she'd summoned him with her thoughts, Odo appeared in front of her. She'd never even heard his footsteps.

His mule-brown hair stuck to his sweating forehead, and the moonlight cast an eerie glow over his chiseled features. He grinned, then struck her. Hard.

She hit the damp ground, pain lancing through her jaw and the taste of blood on her lip. A boot kicked into her middle, sending bile up her throat, acrid and uncontrollable. Coughing, she swallowed it down and scrambled to get her knees under her.

Odo's words were low and vicious. "Foolish woman. Think you're better than me."

A stripe of blue moonlight showed a broken branch beside Odo's muddied boot. She wouldn't be able to best this large man, but she could certainly hit him in the soft bits before he made his cowardly escape. She reached for the branch. The brewer's heel crashed down on her fingers. The dull crack of bone turned Rhianne's stomach as bright pain flashed across her left thumb and forefinger.

He had broken her working hand. She was left-handed, yet another reason half the townspeople threw a fist her way when her uncle wasn't looking.

Tears burned behind her eyes, so she squeezed them shut, gritting her aching jaw to bear the pain in her hand and ribs.

When she opened her eyes, Odo stared down at her, his square jaw tensing and his hands twitching at his sides like he wanted to inflict even more damage than he already had. "Flick those fingers at me again, woman. I dare you."

"You say *woman* like the term is a slight. If I could choose, I'd be born myself every time." She forced the words out. "Try harder with your insults or get out of my way."

Her words earned her another kick. This one turned her inside out. She retched, and her twice-hit rib bone stabbed daggers of pain through her body.

A wolf howled.

It was close. Too close.

Fear cooled Rhianne's pains and held her motionless as

her mind worked. The animal's snarls—hungry and insistent—unspooled her focus on Odo. She knew that howl. It was a scar wolf. Once, the charcoal burner had found a traveling musician whose entire head had been gnawed off by a scar wolf. The bones at the neck had shown the size of the beast's teeth.

A cold like the deepest parts of the river settled over her.

Odo chuckled. "My work is done. I'll let the wolves see if you're more to their taste. You certainly never would have been my choice. I was merely showing you a kindness in offering you a place at my alehouse, filthy, left-handed cow." He pressed the sole of his boot into her broken hand.

Red-hot throbbing writhed through her injury, stealing her breath. Instinct reigning, she cried out. "Uncle Cane!"

But he was still at their workshop in town, his icy demeanor unsuitable for Mabon festivities. If only she could hold her tongue and grow as cold as her uncle, cold as a blade's edge, and hide her emotions from Odo, who fed on her pain. Agony gripped her in another wave and smashed through her senses, making a joke out of her attempts to be stoic.

Spittle flying, Odo crouched, grabbed a handful of dirt and leaves, then shoved the lot of it between her teeth. "Your last meal." His smile showed teeth white as lightning.

Rhianne spit the debris from her mouth, tasting a bitter worm and the metallic tang of blood and earth. Odo's twisted laughter followed him out of the wood.

"I will get my revenge, Odo," she hissed, her words breaking into pieces before they could carry.

Sitting up slowly, she squeezed her eyes shut and took a deep, wrenching breath. A mossy boulder provided support as she hoisted herself to standing. Her injuries screamed, and she took shallow breaths, wanting nothing more than to start this evening over and go back to the dull safety and isolation of her uncle's workshop.

Growling came from the low growth around a turn in the path.

A scar wolf crept into view.

Rhianne's stomach dropped into her shoes.

Silver hair. Black markings across his huge head. Glinting eyes and teeth.

"Uncle! Someone!" Sweat dampened the back of her neck and wet her palms.

She bent to reach for the branch, then managed to curl her unbroken fingers around its jagged end. Hefting it, pain slicing across her middle, she snarled back at the wolf.

"I will not be your supper without a fight."

The animal stepped closer, its steaming breath showing in clouds.

Straightening as best she could, she set her gaze on the wolf.

Fear tightened its grip around her heart. She trembled, teeth clicking together.

Wind whispered through the trees and shook the already dying leaves. The scent of woodsmoke, animal musk, and autumn's leaf mold rose around her face.

The wolf lowered its head.

Then leapt.

Time slowed as the wolf blazed toward her. He was

going to rip her head from her body. Eat her insides before she died.

Shivering, she held up the branch as though it were a pike, then roared like a wild, feral thing.

The wolf landed. The branch dragged across its breast before sliding off target. She turned her grip and pressed the length of it across the wolf's throat to hold him back. Blood ran hot from the tear on the wolf's breast and slicked her hands as the creature's teeth gnashed at her face, its breath hot and stinking as she turned her cheek.

Muscles quaking, Rhianne lost hold of the branch, and it tumbled to the forest floor. She gripped the wolf's bloody, ragged fur, trying to heave him from her chest. Claws raked her middle and down her forearm, but she felt no pain, only the awareness that came with a fight.

CHAPTER 2

WERIAN

The Mabon moon glowed through branches of dark oak, wind-teased maple, and aromatic pine. The trees tipped their boughs respectfully as the Fae Queen's son, Werian, rode his mare toward the Matchweaver's castle.

He'd had that dream again, the one about the strange female with the fierce eyes and the brash tone of voice. It made him...itchy, for lack of a better word. If the Matchweaver could give him some clue as to whether or not this dream female was linked to his fated mate, he wanted that information—mostly because males weren't permitted to ask the Matchweaver for information. Werian grinned, his heart light. Flouting tradition was one of his favorite pastimes.

He straightened his cloak and smoothed his hair around his curling, black horns. The Matchweaver liked a pretty face, and he wasn't above flirting with the evil old gal to get the information he wanted. He could simply dangle his mother's favor in front of her witchy nose, but he preferred to avoid all mention of his mother if it could be helped.

The tang of fresh blood cut the air.

Werian slid from his horse, then ran a hand down the animal's sweat-damp neck. "Go on home, Starblaze. I smell trouble, and that's more my game than yours." Starblaze was a good mare, but she wasn't much for a fight. He needed his best mount for that.

With a quick snort of agreement and a nuzzle against Werian's pointed ear, Starblaze trotted back into the moonlit forest, heading toward the Agate Court, where servants who knew the horse would clean the day's travel off her. Werian rarely stayed at court these days, preferring his own makeshift kingdom aboard a stolen pirate ship near the Sea's Claw, just east of here. Court was his mother's favored domain. Not his. But Starblaze wouldn't mind the politics.

Lifting his sensitive, fae nose, he once again smelled blood and now bile too. And a human who had to be very close indeed. He loved humans. They were far more interesting than his own kind.

A growl thundered beyond plumes of silver fog.

Werian cocked an eyebrow. A scar wolf would provide some fascinating entertainment. The beasties loved a good chase through the wood. But was the wolf the one who had made this nearby human bleed?

Clicking his tongue at a potential naughty scar wolf, Werian frowned and strolled around a curve in the path.

A woman lay on the ground, dress askew, pale arms reaching for something. It was this female's blood that had been spilled. Not much of it. But her presence oozed panic and pain.

Werian opened his mouth to ask if he could give aid, but the scar wolf shot from the shadows. The beast snarled and jumped onto the woman, who wisely snagged a broken branch and jammed it between herself and the wolf's shaggy chest. This scar wolf wasn't like the conditioned ones the enemy Wylfen trained; he could potentially communicate with this one.

Blood ringing through his veins, Werian raced over and slammed a shoulder into the naughty beastie. The wolf yelped, crashed into the ground, then rolled against a pine. But he wasn't down long. He rose onto all fours, lip curling up over his glistening, sharp teeth.

"Easy, beastie." Werian showed the wolf his fae fangs. They were smaller, but no less deadly. The woman warmed his side, where she lay completely still. He did truly hope she wasn't dead. "Go on, friend," he said, whispering to the wolf in its own tongue while he tried to touch its mind with the urge to flee.

The wolf's mind felt scattered and blurry. Werian's heart beat a quick rhythm. If the wolf raged at him, he'd have to kill it, and he really didn't want to. After all, the wolves had been here first, even before the fae. The wolf lowered its head further, then a vicious growling bark snapped from its mouth. Werian's skin turned to gooseflesh, pebbling in waves down his forearms.

The woman stirred. Werian wanted to turn around and check on her, but he couldn't break his focus.

Holding his breath, Werian spread his fingers wide. His kind could speak to animals; the creatures tended to listen far more often to fae than to humans or even elves. "Go, friend. Find a different meal."

The wolf snarled, then turned and sped away.

Exhaling in a rush, Werian spun to see whom he had saved this fine Mabon night.

He bent to study the woman, who had apparently lost consciousness after all she'd been through. The pale rose of her eyelids matched a spring sunrise, and she had rather lovely curves. Poor thing had been through quite a bit. He knelt and shifted her into his arms. She was lighter than he'd expected and was a wonderful balance of strong, sturdy muscles gained from manual labor and soft, pliant flesh that smelled delightfully feminine. His lips twitched as he wondered what that skin might feel like beneath a kiss.

He used the sparkling power of fae healing to mend the human female's broken bones and ripped flesh. Shifting her slightly, warm blood met his hand. His heart caught in his chest. Blood flowed from a large tear on her shoulder, and her lips went blue. Werian shook his head, grimacing. This blood loss was more than he could manage. More than anyone could manage. She would die.

He swallowed. Unless...

The darkness tried to hide the path that led to the Matchweaver's castle, but he knew it was there. He'd visited often before the old witch goddess began attacking people he loved. But the Matchweaver was the only one with magic powerful enough to possibly heal this brave and beautiful woman. If he made a deal with the witch, perhaps she'd try to save this human.

Lifting her gently but swiftly, he headed into the fog

and toward the Matchweaver's castle. As he hurried, his gaze strayed to the human's face and clothing. Something about her piqued his curiosity.

Her soft dress was of a simple weave and dotted with patches and new holes, the hem worn. But her shoes were sound and well-crafted, if not fashionable. A cobbler perhaps? She wore not a speck of jewelry. She was apparently poor, but her brow proud—it made him think of golden crowns and the queens of old.

He held her dirtied fingers in his. "What magic sleeps in your veins, fair wolf fighter?"

The small sound of her lips parting brought his attention to her face.

She looked at him. *Through* him.

His chest seized with shock.

Those eyes.

Determination blazed in their multicolored depths, but before he could look closer to see if he might be seeing what he thought he might be seeing, the woman drifted away again.

Not sparing a moment, he rushed over the autumn's crisp, fallen leaves—running as best he could with her in his arms—to the castle. Perhaps the Matchweaver would also answer a new question: could this human be the woman he had seen in his dreams?

CHAPTER 3
RHIANNE

F ever dreams washed through Rhianne's mind as she slept.

In her dreams, a dark figure blurred across her vision, slamming a wolf to the ground. The dark figure—a man, perhaps—crouched where the wolf had fallen, his arms outstretched and his fingers splayed. Ebony-swathed sparks—like lightning within dark storm clouds—flashed from his palms. *Magic.* Stars blinked between the crisping edges of the dying leaves, and the scent of foreign spices and petrichor spun through the air. The night's shadows and a curtain of thick hair hid the man, all but the line of a strong jaw that caught the starlight. A gentle hand brushed the hair from her face, and a deep voice rumbled quietly through the night.

"Rest, brave one. We'll meet again."

RHIANNE OPENED HER EYES, HER BODY LEADEN AND

lying on a cot. She felt separated from herself. Had the dreams been real? A stone wall stood beside the bed, cool to the touch and smoothed by age. A large skillet hung from a hook above her head. The blanket under her fingers was soft and finely woven. Vision blurry, she squinted at what appeared to be a window where stars twinkled above the sun's final glow of the day.

Two voices filled the air—one melodious and female, the other deep and lilting with an odd accent. She sat up and wished she hadn't. Her head felt like a ball of poorly spun wool. Bandages swathed her left arm, hand, and shoulder, her pulse and the heat of pain beating dully underneath.

The wolf had been real.

The night came rushing back, and she clutched at the blanket with weak and aching fingers. As she winced, pinches of pain lashed her face. Scratches marred her cheeks, and she touched them gingerly. A feeling like a thousand needle pricks pressed her torso where the wolf's claws had slashed the skin and where Odo's boot had landed. Her stomach clenched against the sensation. But she should have been in more pain.

Her eyes shuttered, and for a while, she dreamed once more.

The solid *thunk* of a closing door sounded far away, waking her.

Still abed, Rhianne studied the room. In the center of what was clearly a kitchen, a fire crackled in a circle of stones—an old-style hearth under a vented hole in the ceiling. A gnarled woman stirred the contents of a large cauldron. She was so tall that her head brushed the dried yarrow hanging from a ceiling hook. The woman wore her hair in a thick braid, coiled on top of her head, and Rhianne marveled at its color. The green of spring grass, brighter than any noblewoman's ring.

Rhianne gripped the blanket. This was the witch, the Matchweaver, the woman who had cursed and battled Princess Aurora and Prince Filip, the mercurial goddess who held the kingdom's love matches in her very hands.

As Rhianne's mind warred over what to say first, her attention strayed back to the witch's hair. The other maidens who had visited the witch and returned to town had mentioned the color, but Rhianne hadn't truly considered how amazing it would be. She had been too concerned with the possibility of finding her own match. But here, now, the witch's shockingly bright hair swallowed all else and veritably shouted *Here is magic!*

"What are you gaping at, girl?" The witch scowled.

"Mistress Matchweaver," Rhianne said, her voice shaking from what her body had endured and the fear she held of this magical person. "Thank you for permitting me to enter your home. I hope it's not rude to mention, but your hair fascinates me. It's lovely." There. That was a compliment. A solid start. Who didn't like having their hair praised? Rhianne truly wanted to mention how terrible it was that the witch had done what she had to the princess, but she was here now and would get what she needed from the Matchweaver—a husband, a partner, someone to help her keep food on the table and fire in the hearth. "The color... It's beyond, well, I don't know. But it is beyond anything I could have imagined."

"Not beyond words though, it seems." The witch

stirred the pot. "Waking every being from here to the Sea's Claw."

A day's walk from the edge of the Forest of Illumahrah, the Sea's Claw was where all freshwater creeks and rivers came together to pour into the ocean's wild world.

"Thank you for saving me." Rhianne lifted a tied bunch of sage that had been tucked beneath her pillow. What was this used for? Simple air cleansing? Or for a spell? After sniffing its lovely scent, she released it into the Matchweaver's outstretched hand. "Did you use magic on me? If so, thank you twice over."

The witch accepted the sage. "Ah. Wondered where I had left today's bunch. You were attacked days ago. In exchange for a fine piece of spirit agate, I did use magic to help you heal, but I wasn't the one who saved you in the wood, girl."

"My name is Rhianne, if you please."

With a sniff, the witch muttered, "Fine manners from a cobbler's daughter."

"He is my uncle."

"Who is?"

"The cobbler. My parents died long ago." Rhianne narrowed her eyes. "I would've guessed you'd know that. With all due respect."

The witch's body froze. Her gaze lashed out like a nine-tailed whip. "The loom only shows a match. It doesn't play out the entire world's goings-on."

Rhianne lowered her gaze. "Apologies, Mistress Matchweaver. I didn't mean to offend." *Please don't decide to curse me. I don't have the power of a water mage or a handsome elven warrior at my side.* "I am so grateful for your help and for your willingness to accept me here. I worried you would turn me away because I'm older than most maidens. It would be well within reason, so once again, thank you very much. Perhaps, before you find me a match, I can help you around the castle in exchange for your healing magic."

"We'll see," the witch said begrudgingly. A smile teased the side of her mouth. The wooden spoon she used boasted silver runes along its handle.

Rhianne squinted in the low light as she tried to see the curls of magical script more clearly. "Who *did* save me, and, if I may ask, what spell are you concocting just now?"

Curiosity flung Rhianne's mind from one thing to another like a windstorm knocking a leaf about. She longed to study every corner of the room and ask every question she could think of, to tuck the information away for later use or for survival. She was a curious sort, but even though her questions were always practical, her uncle told her to shut up at least once a day. It never took.

A leek went into the cauldron. "This is no spell," the witch said. "This, my dear, is supper. And the one who saved you is beyond your ken, human."

Beyond her ken? What did that mean? "A noble, then?" Rhianne asked. "Hunting here? I would've thought you yourself had full run of the place, Mistress." Rhianne thought no such thing, in truth. King Athellore had ordered the Matchweaver to remain in the wood. She was a prisoner. But Rhianne wasn't a fool. She wasn't about to say anything about that and find herself bound in magic.

That whiplike gaze snapped out again. "I do, as you say, have the run of the place. But the fae ride through as they choose. With my good wishes. Their home is not far from here, magically speaking."

Rhianne's heart thumped hard against the base of her throat. Then the memory of the dark figure in the forest came flooding into her mind. The quick movements. The black-swathed sparks. Warm arms and whispered spells.

"A fae helped me fight off the wolf." It was unbelievable. A cobbler's niece rescued by a fae. A wide smile pulled at the scratches on her cheeks. She had joined forces with a dashing fae warrior. Amazing.

"Yes." The Matchweaver's face twisted like she'd smelled something foul. "The fae deigned to preserve your little life."

Rhianne would have to think of a way to thank him. "If I may ask... How does one show gratitude to a fae for helping one fight off a scar wolf?"

Hand on a hip, with the spoon dripping onto the flagstone floor, the Matchweaver eyed Rhianne. "You believe he merely helped you defeat the wolf?" The witch shook her head and ladled out a steaming bowl for Rhianne.

Rhianne accepted the warm, wooden bowl. "Well, I did manage to injure the beast as it struck me," she said tentatively, "but I would've been dead without the fae's aid. I don't mean to say I wouldn't be torn to shreds. Is the fae here still? May I thank him?"

Her mind tumbled from image to image as she guessed how tall he might be, what color his eyes held, and whether or not he had the thick, curling horns that some talked about seeing on noble fae during the battles with the Wylfen.

With a word of thanks, Rhianne tucked into her onion soup. It was very good.

The spoon knocked against the cauldron as the Matchweaver muttered something about humans. "Tell me, proud girl, why do you believe humans are worth my time at the Mageloom?"

Sweat beaded on Rhianne's upper lip. If she answered in a displeasing way, would the witch decide to keep the loom from humans? If Rhianne's next words turned the witch's heart from humans, none would find their partners for life. That's what she'd always been told anyway. Rhianne had to choose her answer carefully, to prove that humans were worth the witch's trouble, that humans were to be respected in their own way.

She set her bowl on her cot, beside her folded legs. "Most humans must survive without magic." Swallowing, she forced herself to meet the witch's gaze and show the earnest belief she held. "We average humans must be the toughest when you compare non-magical humans, human witches, human water mages, elves, and fae. We need all the help we can get." Her heart pounded, making her injuries throb.

"Your thoughts on the hierarchy of beings within our realm and the next do not anger me, affect me, or change me. Speak exactly as you like."

But Rhianne didn't buy the witch's apathy. She'd certainly been ready to go to war against the king for the slight of a betrothal without her consent.

The witch began muttering as she waved a willow-branch wand to tidy up the kitchen. "You are one of a thousand. So many human girls... And their heads full of only one thing. Their own small lives. I do suppose," the Matchweaver said, now slurping a portion of soup, "there is beauty in the small lives. Life requires all, high and low, complicated and simple, to turn the wheel of time. Now, finish your supper, and I'll read my loom for you before you talk my ears into crawling up the sides of my head and hiding in this hair you like so much."

Mostly healed but still tender in many spots, Rhianne ignored the dull jabs and aches of her freshly mended injuries and hurried to gulp down the last of her soup. The witch led her into a circular chamber. Windows of leaded and colored glass marked each of the four directions. Blue for north. Red for west. Green for south. Purple for east. Though the sun had set hours ago, light danced through the windows as if the stars themselves had descended from the heavens to dwell in the wood's ancient castle.

The Mageloom was a riot of light and dark, muted and saturated colors. Every hue under the sun stretched and ducked and threaded its way from one end of the black wood frame to the other. The weaving refused to show anything to anyone except the witch, of course, but Rhianne couldn't help studying the wool, searching for a face, a hand, any clue to who might be her match for life.

The witch sat in a willow-branch chair that evoked illusions of antlers and tentacles. With movements as practiced as any master craftsman, the Matchweaver thrust the shuttle through, then beat the weave down. Legends said there had been just five Matchweavers, chosen by the magic of the castle, chosen for their affinity with Seeing.

"*Hmm.*" The witch's wrinkled fingers played over the

weaves as she muttered something about the moon. "I see you."

Rhianne's heart beat too quickly. This was it. The announcement she had craved for years. Every night, she'd dreamed of whom he might be, of who might fit her well enough to live a contented, simple life. And now, the moment had arrived. She stepped forward, then back again, afraid if she came too close to the witch's elbow, she might disrupt the magic.

The stones under her shoes trembled.

With a start, she glanced down, but there was nothing to see.

Nerves. That was all. She shook her head to clear it. The castle was not about to crumble around her head.

"Yes, I see you, Rhianne the cobbler. Practical. Outspoken."

The witch laughed quietly, her mouth tucking up into her cheeks. Then she turned and reached out to touch Rhianne's chin. The Matchweaver inhaled, slow and concerned. What did the witch see in her face?

"You've not had it easy, have you?" the witch asked, her voice kinder now than it had been. How could she be kind when she had been so evil to Princess Aurora? Rhianne almost wished the witch were more predictable. If the Matchweaver were consistently terrible, Rhianne could have planned out answers to probable questions, but this mercurial nature was unsettling and horribly frightening.

Was the loom showing one of the many times Odo had thrown Rhianne to the ground? The instances of slapping from other women? How the men pinched at Rhianne's backside, then spit as she kicked out at their fingers, all while they called her demon or left-handed cow?

None of that was her fault. She hadn't started a war that had kept her from finding a match. She hadn't asked to be born with a more capable left hand than right. The village was packed with ignorant folk, and she refused to be ashamed of what she'd endured.

Her jaw tightened. "I manage."

"The other humans do not see you as ideal, *hmm*."

"I am a hard worker and never set out to start any fights. I do hope the loom shows a match that befits me, because I can't agree to wed a mean sort or a layabout. I want someone with potential. I'll challenge him, help him rise. And he can do the same for me."

Crossing her arms and facing the loom, the witch tilted her head and watched her visions in the weaving. "Whoever he is, he would be best born deaf," she muttered, then her hand shot out toward the rainbow wool. "No." She stood suddenly, then stumbled backward, kicking her chair with her heel.

To keep the Matchweaver from falling, Rhianne grabbed her arm.

The witch jerked away and eyed her wildly. "It can't be you. I will not have it. He deserves a noblewoman at the very least. She will loathe me for this! Ride me to the underworld with a crowd of ravenous hounds! No!"

Rhianne stepped away to avoid the mad witch, but the old woman caught her sleeve and jerked her closer. "Who will loathe you?" Rhianne asked.

The witch's rheumy eyes rolled. "Do you have fae blood and concealed it, child?"

But the witch didn't wait for an answer. Her fingernail lashed out and cut Rhianne's thumb, quicker than an angry cat. The witch tasted her blood, then she spat it out.

"You have none. Go. Get out! You have pissed on my lightning bolt, you have, and I can't stand the sight of you. Go!"

The witch shoved Rhianne through the room where they'd had supper, then across a threshold into a courtyard where the autumn wind whipped leaves through the night air.

"Please!" Rhianne dipped a panicked bow. "I'm so sorry—"

Wailing unintelligibly, the Matchweaver pushed her. Rhianne landed on a straw-lined path beside a chaotic garden boasting leaves so tall they nearly blocked out the moon's light.

"Feed the goats, girl," the witch spat, "and do not come to me until I call."

The witch hauled herself inside and slammed the door, fleeing like Rhianne had the royal army at her back.

CHAPTER 4
WERIAN

Walking past two well-armored guards who bowed low, Werian entered the Agate Palace. He hoped against all the hope in the great, grand world that he would somehow avoid seeing his mother, the Fae Queen. Birch trees lined the candlelit foyer where courtiers were drinking lavender wine and playing the ancient dice game of Trap. Flaxen-haired Wynflaed wore a crown of berries slung low around her small, pointed horns. She laughed, the sound like wind chimes, as she whispered to Isen, whose dark countenance lightened a fraction.

"If you're making Isen happy," he said to Wynflaed in passing, "I don't even want to know what you're up to, cousin."

Wynflaed snagged his sleeve, her lips dark with berry juice. The courtiers bowed and curtseyed to Werian, their gazes clinging. "Join us," Wynflaed pleaded. "Please?"

"Not tonight."

Isen shifted away, his long, silver hair covering his face, and rolled the dice to the cheers of the others. "We see so little of you these days, Prince Werian," he said.

"Ah, you know me." Werian began to walk away. "I'm only content when I'm riding."

"Wine, Your Majesty?" Bathilda presented a cup and a smile that said she was offering far more than a drink.

"No, thank you." He made certain his expression said he knew exactly what she wanted to do with the rest of this long, long night. "That particular wine is not to my liking. Perhaps try my mother's consort? I've heard he appreciates a sour grape."

Her mouth popped open, and before she could retort or ply, Werian bowed, then hurried onward, aiming for his chambers in the back of the ancient palace. Dodging four other fae's attempts to draw him into dark corners for an embrace or a game of dice, he finally made it and shut his door firmly. At the far end of his sitting room, a row of embroidered and bedecked cloaks that brought out the purple strands in his hair and the ebony of his large horns hung on brass hooks. He set a palm against the panel hidden behind the cloaks, almost missing the feel of his finest clothing. He couldn't wear his best when he posed as one Captain Shadowhood, mysterious pirate of Sea's Claw and purveyor of spirit agate and the bane of the fae court. He had to remain unknown, or all the fun would end in one furious lady who would most certainly have his head despite the fact that he was her only child.

Behind the cloaks, the secret door swung open, and Werian slipped inside. The Matchweaver's cackling echoed through his mind as he recalled their conversation before he'd left the human woman to recover. He'd asked the witch if the injured woman might be his match, mentioning that he'd dreamed of the woman's exact shade of eye color. The witch had thought it preposterous, which of course, it was. Werian still believed it might be true.

"No, no, my prince," the witch had said. "I'll match you with another fae of high birth. Or perhaps some witch previously hidden from my senses. The loom and I will find you a great one, I'm certain. Your mother will be pleased. She has long searched for the right bride for you, hasn't she? I saw you in my loom. I saw you, and I will see your match within the next few nights. That is how it goes."

Werian removed a golden key from a chain he always wore around his neck and unlocked a chest filled with spirit agate pieces that were small enough to be smuggled out of fae territory under his mother's arrogant, selfish nose. She refused to sell the magical stones that increased the power of any who had magic in their blood. And so he stole them, sold them, then gave the garnered coin to those who needed it the most, the humans struggling to eke out a living in the eastern province where local taxes were fully ridiculous. He had buried a large stash of spirit agate—glamoured to look like ancient wine amphorae— near Loreton Palace. But he didn't need to travel that far to find a temptation for the witch. From his wooden chest, he selected a fine, palm-sized agate, its glittering insides showing crystals that reminded him of dragon spikes. He tossed it up, then pocketed the magical stone, its power a remnant of the Source's spring that had long ago disappeared under the forest floor. This nice piece would be agate enough to persuade the Matchweaver to spout information like a fountain.

A chime sounded in the main area of his chamber. Werian's heart stuttered, and he hurriedly slipped out of the secret room, shutting the door firmly. He walked into the dark near his bed and table.

"What are you doing back there in the shadows, my darling son?"

As usual, his stomach twisted at the sound of the Fae Queen's voice. By the gods, how he hated her. "Just deciding which cloak would look best after hours. I wanted to examine my new blue one by the light of the moon through the window."

"Of course," she purred.

It was almost worse that the woman was kind to him and no other. He wanted her to strike out directly and have the fight they never seemed quite ready to commence. Or did he? He truly wasn't certain what he wanted. For her to stop hoarding her wealth? To cease the new moon festivities that involved tempting humans to a week-long celebration he was fairly certain they never would attend if not for the dangerous lure of fae beauty? Yes and yes.

She came close, her gown swishing along the marble tiles, the beads sewn into her hem rattling like a wood snake's tail. He heard her inhale.

"You smell like the forest. You spend so much time in the oaks, I feel I made a mistake in naming you. I should've called you Robin."

"If you could stand to wear trousers," he said, "you'd like the view from the high branches. It's serene and rather stunning." They shared a love of all things beautiful, but that was where their similarities ended.

She laughed easily, pleased at his attention, and he hated the small part of himself that enjoyed it. A son was never truly free from a parent, no matter how terrible. He was reminded of the time ten years back when she'd hired a pirate to kidnap a younger princess of Khem for a variety of unsavory reasons. Thankfully, the lady had escaped his evil mother's plan.

He touched the golden key beneath his tunic and tried to ignore the pain of old grievances. The piece of spirit agate warmed his skin through his trouser pocket.

"I am to bed, Mother. Do you need anything else?"

"Bed? Alone? This early?"

"I'm not nearly the rogue you wish I were."

"I would see you here at the palace more often and less in the trees, Robin." Her grin showed teeth, and she'd meant the new nickname to bite. It didn't.

"I'd rather be a robin than a pointless peacock."

She barked an unbecoming laugh and swept from the room. "One would guess you hate who you are, my son," she said, her voice trailing off as her footsteps faded into silence.

But he didn't. Not exactly. He hated that not everyone had the fae level of wealth. The luxury his family possessed would always far outdo anything the common folk had in the human lands of Lore. It was part of being fae and of the fae court. But the vast divide of having and being without didn't have to stretch as wide as it did. It was his only desire to lessen that break and ease the pain of the lean children he glimpsed in his time as Captain Shadowhood.

As soon as he was certain his mother was long gone, off to the dancing and the feasting, he strolled out a side door, past the barn and the multitude of cats Princess Aurora had loved when she was young, and rode his finest stallion back to the Matchweaver, her castle, and the woman who might just be the answer to the question that was his life.

CHAPTER 5

RHIANNE

In the castle's inner courtyard, Rhianne recovered from the witch's shove and stood, legs shaking as the chill wind stirred the scent of lavender from the garden. She hurt all over. Had she just lost her chance at finding a partner? By the Goddess Vahly, she truly wished she didn't care about a husband. But her heart wanted a close companion. Loneliness was the weighty cloak she was more than ready to throw off her shoulders.

In the rosy glow of twilight, a lantern bobbed across the grounds, held by one of two women who were leading a stomping horse to its stall for the night. A third woman emptied a bucket into a small trench beside an outbuilding before pulling her kerchief from her hair and heading up a set of stairs with a weary gait.

Rhianne shook her head. No one seemed alarmed at the witch's outburst. Perhaps her anger got the best of her regularly.

But how could Rhianne's match be so horrible that it

made the witch shut herself into the keep in such a mad frenzy? Rhianne was no princess. What about the match could possibly be so important to the witch?

One of the women who'd settled the horse walked up with two buckets in her hands. She was about Rhianne's age, and her hair was the same pale yellow as the straw at their feet. Mud caked the woman's knuckles, and a clod of the same tangled a spot above her ear.

"You must be matched to a truly fine man." The woman eyed the two doors at the back of the keep—one led to the kitchen and the other to the loom's chamber. "Don't worry. She'll come around. She thinks we village folk should never get a man with any kind of noble blood, no matter how poor their families have become over the centuries. Sometimes I wish we had one of the earlier Matchweavers. Stories say the last one was kind." She thrust a pail of seedpods at Rhianne. "I'm Melianor. But that's too much of a mouthful for a gal like me, so you can call me Nor for short."

Rhianne studied Nor's face, searching for a clue as to whether the woman was happy here or not. She wondered what had pushed Nor into remaining here. "I hope you're right about the witch. I'm Rhianne."

The path they walked led into a two-story barn where goats gathered to lip the edges of their pails. The musky scent of manure and damp alfalfa fought for dominance in the ancient structure. Nor cupped handfuls of seedpods and fed them to the animals. Rhianne, who hated idleness, joined in.

"I guess you're one of the women who didn't like her match and decided to stay here and work at the castle?"

She glanced at Nor, hoping her question wasn't too nosy. It was nice talking to someone who was kind to her for a change.

"I am. I don't blame the witch, of course. She only sees the match. The loom makes the decision. I traveled to the village where my match lives and made a go of it. Lasted a sennight. But pretty quick, I realized I'd rather spend a lifetime snuggling up to Fat Billy than to my match."

"Does the Matchweaver approve of your relationship with this Fat Billy fellow?"

Nor barked a laugh and pointed to a goat behind her. His legs were like tree trunks, and his belly was wide as Nor's outstretched arms. "Allow me to introduce Master Billy."

Rhianne chuckled, then curtseyed to the big goat. "Good evening." She faced Nor again, uneasy about her own prospects. "What was so bad about your match?"

"The loom showed Toma from Grey's Ridge. Maybe he was a good one before he lost his first wife, but grief twisted him into a drunk who loves to shout eviscerating insults. Unfortunately for him, I don't enjoy living at the receiving end of his favorite pastime. I returned, and the witch kindly did a second reading." Nor grinned and wiggled her eyebrows. "Turns out, Toma's second favorite pastime—eating overly rich foods—will take him down in the spring. The Matchweaver and I decided it might be a good idea if I showed up on his doorstep to marry him the day winter breaks."

Smart. "Just in time to take his fine fields before he dies, eh?"

"Indeed."

They tossed the last of the seedpods to the goats, then set the pails by the water trough. Nor walked Rhianne back to the garden, where they began to pick moonblooms. The stories said the witch bathed in the violet flowers to increase her powers.

Though the night breeze was pleasant and Rhianne's injuries weren't too painful, doubts tore at her mind like the scar wolf's claws. Was her match an evil man? Or was he an enemy of the witch? What could it be?

Rhianne sighed, brushing her finger over the moonblooms' velvet petals before picking them. If only there were a way to work out this problem besides leaving the witch alone to think. Maybe she could be persuaded to at least allow Rhianne to speak to the man. If she only knew his name, she could find him herself and see what could be done. But she was at the mercy of the witch and her whims. No one forced a sorceress to do their bidding.

Nor plucked the blooms expertly, three to Rhianne's one. "Your match might be wonderful. It could be that the Matchweaver is angry because your match doesn't line up with her latest scheme. Her goal in life is to be invited to the fae court though she'd never admit it. Now that Princess Aurora and Prince Filip's relationship is settled, she wants everyone to return to worshipping her properly," Nor said, rolling her eyes. "She is mad with the need for the upper crust to regard her as a goddess. The witch's opinion of herself is larger than the skies."

"Considering what she did to Princess Aurora, I seriously doubt she'll ever be invited anywhere."

"True," Nor said. She glanced over her shoulder. "The witch isn't very level-headed."

"I noticed."

"She probably thinks she can magic or manipulate her way back into the good graces of Lore's upper class."

Rhianne snorted. "Good luck to her on that." The king of Lore had banished the witch here for what she'd done. It was amazing that he hadn't had her put to death.

"Now the fae...I don't know how they feel about her," Rhianne said. Maybe the witch wanted to please a noble family and reap the benefits. Rhianne's match to said family's son would ruin any goodwill the witch could hope for.

Nor shrugged. "I've no idea about the fae. I try to stay within my own simple life and avoid the grander plots and paths." She leaned close and whispered, "Our witch goddess is a grasping, frightening being. But I can't say she hasn't cared for me, allowing me to stay here."

"Indeed," Rhianne agreed.

Nor brushed her dress free of leaves, then waved Rhianne toward a set of stairs leading up the western wall of the castle. The stone steps were worn by ages of comings and goings, their middles dipped like soup bowls. Nor led Rhianne into a dark room built into the curtain wall. They placed the moonblooms beside a set of shelves stacked with crockery, then returned to the stairs. Rhianne wondered if the witch used all of these stores herself or if she knew others like herself, born to work the magic of runes, herbs, and wands given by the Sacred Oak.

"Are there any other witches nearby?" Others existed in the kingdom and beyond, but none had been overly praised.

"I don't think so." Nor took a lantern from a shelf at

the base of the stairs and lit the wick with a flint and striker she had in a small bag at her belt.

"I wonder, then, if the witch wants to visit the fae court for the pleasure of other magical beings' company."

As they stepped down into the courtyard, Nor plucked an errant moonbloom leaf from Rhianne's hair. Rhianne's heart softened at the gentle touch.

"I think the witch would be disappointed if the fae merely provided understanding company." Nor held the lantern so that its lemon-hued light painted their path. The day's glowing farewell had faded, and night claimed the beginning of its reign. "Our witch desires laud and fame. Bowing and gasps upon her blessed arrival. A fae prince rode by here the night the witch saved you from the mist."

The Matchweaver's explanation, as well as the low, accented voice in the kitchen, flashed through Rhianne's mind, sparking excitement like she had a lantern of her own hiding deep within her soul.

"The witch didn't save me," she explained. "The fae helped me fight off a scar wolf."

"Truly?" Nor raised both eyebrows as they passed the garden and came to a well in the center of the courtyard. Rhianne took the lantern so Nor could retrieve the bucket. "I had thought the fae were above rescuing human maidens."

Then one word Nor had said sank in. *Prince.* The lantern slipped from Rhianne's grip, but she grabbed it before it fell. "Did you say he was a royal?"

A smile broke across Nor's face as she lowered the bucket into the well. "Yes. The Fae Queen's only son. I've heard he is strikingly handsome but a complete rogue." She raised the bucket back up, water sloshing over the side.

Rhianne swallowed. It had been shocking enough that a fae had saved her, but the Prince of the Fae Court?

Nor touched her shoulder. "Are you all right?"

"I can't believe I fought alongside a fae prince. *The* Fae Prince."

"Alongside?" Nor stood with the dripping bucket perched on the side of the well, regarding Rhianne with wide eyes. "Impressive. I bet that's why he helped you. Because you showed courage." Nor took a wooden cup from a nail on the underside of the well's small roof and scooped some water to drink. "Now, take a good sip, and then I'll show you where you can sleep for the night. In exchange, you can tell me the story of your battle with the wolf."

The goats bleated quietly from the barn as Rhianne told the tale outside the double doors.

"And then the fae appeared, just a dark shape in the wood. He was tall and quick, but it was full night by then, and I couldn't see much. He threw the wolf off of me, then I believe he spoke to the animal and persuaded it to flee. That's all I can remember."

Nor huffed a breath. "It's too bad you had so much blood loss. I would've liked a better description of the prince in action. I bet it was breathtaking to see a fae as lovely as him working magic and fighting off such a vicious beast."

The light of excitement flared hotly inside Rhianne. "We are agreed on that," she said, her voice a bit breathless.

She too would've loved to have seen more of him and his otherworldly skills.

A tiny goat trotted out of the darkness from the general direction of the barn. Nor lifted the animal into her arms.

A scent like Naroniti spices drifted from the depths of the forest beyond the castle.

"I can finish the story, if you like," a deep voice said.

The women whirled, and Rhianne's heart tripled its pace.

A male fae stood beyond the well, near the stables, his head cocked to the side and a grin playing over his full lips.

Was this the one who had helped her?

He was taller than the witch, who towered over most. The breeze tousled the fae's blackberry-hued hair, and curling horns showed between the waves of thick locks. His horns were like a ram's, cresting back, over his head, and she had the oddest desire to run a finger down the length of them and watch how the touch affected him.

Warmth traveled from her chest to her neck like a palm brushing up her body.

The fae's face was full of mischief as he met her gaze. His dark eyes seemed to say *I dare you.*

Her hands curled into the thin fabric of her dress.

A silver clasp held a dark cloak at his strong neck. Underneath, a leather vest lay against his chest, pressing against muscle and bone, and a sword hung from the belt at his narrow waist. Runes similar to those on the witch's ladle decorated the weapon's hilt, as well as a golden disc he wore on a chain. Black boots came to points—like his ears—and tipped up at the ends.

"Are you finished taking it all in?" He waved a hand as if presenting himself.

Rhianne's stomach fluttered, and her cheeks blazed. If only her mouth would work. She couldn't seem to form words. It was no surprise. She had no idea how to speak to a noble fae—or any noble for that matter. A cobbler had no interactions with such folk.

The fae sketched a shallow bow, and Nor laughed in quick surprise, covering her mouth as she dipped a clumsy curtsey.

"I am Werian of the Agate Court," he said with that lovely, accented voice of his, the same voice she'd heard before waking properly in the witch's kitchen. "I do hope you are mending quickly." His gaze took in the scratches on Rhianne's face and her bandages.

Perhaps Rhianne could simply say *Good evening*. But that lacked the proper regard. He had saved her life, given her aid against the scar wolf purely out of honor or kindness or something of the sort. As far as she knew, he had received no reward. Fidgeting with her dress, she sighed and gathered her churning thoughts. The starry sky created a silver silhouette of his horns and the sweep of his hair.

"We meet again, fellow warrior," she said. "High Prince, thank you for your aid in the wood."

Werian closed his eyes briefly in acknowledgment, his black lashes like a raven's feather on his strong cheekbones. His elegant fingers gripped his sword's hilt.

Imagine. The cobbler's niece greeting the Fae Prince.

Maybe she didn't even need a match. Life was throwing

her such adventures just beyond her small village. Why go back?

The fae reached toward Nor. "May I?"

He glanced at the baby goat, and though Nor narrowed her eyes, she nodded.

Brushing the tuft of hair between the goat's ears, he said to Rhianne, "You displayed great bravery. Most humans fall to threads at the sight of a scar wolf. I'm more than willing to venture into the wilds of the enchanted forest and beyond with you. If you ever feel the urge to explore, that is."

He was clearly being overly kind in an effort to flatter her. Of course he couldn't possibly mean it. Perhaps making outlandish plans was a fae thing to do. Regardless, this was all too exciting to worry about acting the fool.

She stepped forward, daring to reach for the fae's sword and lifting her eyebrows in question. "May I see your blade?"

"Rhianne," Nor hissed. "She'll be watching. This will not please her." Nor's gaze darted to the window above the Matchweaver's great hall.

Venturing into the wilds with a fae was exactly what Rhianne wanted, although she had never realized it before now. How could she ever have thought to be content making boots and shoes for an entire lifetime and suffering the glare of stupid Odo? Perhaps her strange dreams were not the stuff of silly nonsense or madness. Perhaps this fae prince was serious about the idea of adventure.

Her life had only just started. Today. Now.

Werian handed her the sword, hilt first.

The steel was a luminous black—like a beetle's wings.

She stared at it, half expecting the weapon to disappear and for her to realize this was all a dream.

Her gaze snapped to Werian's face, and her breath caught in her chest like a trapped bird. Was he the one from her dreams?

"The witch won't like this, Rhianne. Not at all," Nor whispered.

Werian shrugged. "I don't follow her rules. But if you wish for me to leave, I will. I wouldn't want to cause difficulties you'd rather avoid."

Nor mumbled an apology. "No, of course not."

As Rhianne turned the blade back and forth to catch the starlight, she felt her heart open to the idea of a life she had never thought would happen. She met the fae's eyes, forcing her desire for a new path through her look.

"My name is Rhianne, and I would love nothing more than to enjoy some adventure with you. But first, I should hear what the witch has to say about my potential match."

"Certainly," he said before launching into the conclusion of the tale that she couldn't recall. "Your friend here injured the scar wolf," he said to Nor. "The creature was weak by the time I arrived. I shouldered him to the ground, off Rhianne." His face turned to her, his eyes glinting as he said her name. "Then I spoke a spell of caution to the animal so I didn't have to kill him."

Nor's narrowed eyes softened, and she smiled. "That was kind." Her cheeks darkened, and her eyes moved left to right like her mind was working over a problem. "What if Rhianne's match sends her far away from here? Will you search her out?"

Heat poured over Rhianne's neck and face, and she

glared at Nor out of the corner of her eye. "I'm sure Prince Werian will do as he pleases. Now, if you'll excuse us, High Prince, we are to bed." She returned his sword as Nor nodded and yawned.

"Of course." He sheathed his weapon with a movement too fast to see. "Sleep well, warrior."

Rhianne had to rip her gaze from him to follow Nor toward the outbuilding near the castle's back wall— presumably the sleeping quarters. When Rhianne peered over her shoulder to catch one last glimpse, he was already gone. Only starlight and shadow remained where he had stood.

CHAPTER 6

WERIAN

As soon as the women turned away, Werian returned to the witch's keep. He swung the door open and said, "Dearest wild goddess witch of the enchanted wood, do share why you're being so hateful to that young woman."

"I..." The crone's voice echoed from her bedchamber, where she undoubtedly stewed behind a locked door. "I am indisposed, Prince."

Werian leaned against the doorframe. He took the piece of spirit agate from his pocket, then tossed it into the air, catching it neatly. "I have a gift for you, Matchweaver. All I ask is that you open this door and tell me what you know of this human." Why did he feel such an incredible urge to find out about Rhianne? She couldn't be the one from his dreams. Surely not. But the Matchweaver was hiding something from him, and he would find out eventually.

"Apologies, Noble Prince. I cannot possibly open that door. I... I am unwell."

"Goddess Lyra bless you, witch," he said through his teeth. The crone deserved a curse in place of any blessing. It was so odd that the Source of magic had given the kingdom of Lore a witch such as this to keep love alive. There was surely some life lesson hidden in the Source's choice, but Werian had no patience to untangle the meaning. He had to get back to his journey to the Sea's Claw. He had a contact waiting to buy more spirit agate, and the man was incredibly difficult to reach. "I will return soon and see how you fare then." He waited for one more moment... Perhaps she would relent. But no.

He left to find his white stallion—Moon—then prepared to leave. He tied his hair back and prepared to glamour himself into Captain Shadowhood. The pounding of hooves halted the tingling magic in his fingers.

Who approached in the middle of night, this far into the enchanted wood?

With fae speed, he slid his bow from the oiled leather bag tied across the back of his saddle and nocked an arrow.

"Prince Werian!" A messenger in Lore livery—a stag over water—and five guards in full armor came riding off the path through the wind-tossed pines.

Werian returned his bow to its case and set the unused arrow in its sling. "This must be quite important to have you flinging yourselves through the Matchweaver's boundary in the middle of the night."

The messenger handed over a sealed scroll. The seal bore the crest of Princess Aurora—Aury to those who knew her well. Deep blue wax showed an *A* set with jagged spikes meant to look like ice, and the crest reminded him of her fight at Dragon Pass, where she had wielded her water mage power beside the fantastically vicious Filip, the second-born elven prince of Balaur.

DEAR COUSIN,

HIS HEART WARMED. HE WAS SO GLAD SHE'D GONE BACK to calling him kin despite the fact that they shared no blood and she now knew it. Aury would always feel like a true cousin to him. In truth, she felt like his only real family. It wasn't as if he were close to his horrid mother. It'd be easier to have a kind relationship with a resurrected corpse with a penchant for eviscerating curses.

I SCRIED YOU AND SENT THIS AS QUICKLY AS HUMANLY possible.

HE GRINNED, KNOWING AURY WAS POKING AT THE FACT that she was not fae, that she had learned she was human not so long ago. Of course, she was no ordinary human. She was a mage who could fight with snow, river, and sea, and she saw visions in water as well.

MY SCRYING BOWL SHOWED YOU SAILING TO KHEM alongside a dark-haired woman. But more importantly, I saw a

dragon circling the harbor at the Sea's Claw and a vision of your
ship wrapped in flames. I can't tell you the timing. Filip and I will
meet you there with Jewel. Be safe, Cousin!

AURY

WERIAN CRUMPLED THE NOTE IN HIS HAND AND DUG HIS
heels into Moon's sides.

His ship could not burn. His loyal crew could be asleep
when the fire took hold. The smoke would easily steal their
fragile, human lives. Plus, it had taken him years to have
the ship built and glamoured. The magic alone had nearly
cost him his life. Without that ship, he wouldn't be able to
trade the agate and help the humans who relied on him. If
he were being honest with himself, the ship was his
freedom from the land where his evil mother could twist
his life and force him into deals that went against every
fiber in his being. Sailing into the great ocean to explore
islands was the best part of his admittedly pretty fantastic
life.

But his crew, his men...

His heart shivered as their faces blinked through his
mind. Little John—despite his harsh coastal accent and
complete lack of style—was like a brother to Werian. He'd
been there every step of the way as Werian had built the
secret spirit agate trade. The man did seem invincible. At
seven feet tall, he defeated human ruffians with ease. He
was better than Werian with the quarterstaff. But dragons
were a different challenge altogether.

He couldn't stand the thought of losing John.

The trees bowed from his path, appearing eager to help him as Moon sped through the forest. Birds and small creatures burst from the undergrowth he blazed past, the galloping steed waking them, frightening them. The forest thinned then opened up into the rolling lands of Lore's eastern province, where the rich grew richer and the poor grew poorer.

He was glad he'd told Aury and Filip about his secret name and what he did at the Sea's Claw. They didn't know everything, but thankfully, he'd told them enough to help him when he needed it.

"Come on, good fellow. Faster now." The autumn wind broke across Werian's cheeks and chin, the scent of the nearby villages' woodsmoke twisting his stomach. Aury's words pricked at his mind. Who was the brunette in her vision? Could it be the cobbler's niece, Rhianne? And why in the name of Arcturus's sacred light would they be sailing to the island of Khem? It was a lovely place but incredibly dangerous. He'd never take someone from a simple Lore village to that island.

Riding through the night, Werian didn't stop once. Rhianne wasn't safe at the Matchweaver's castle while the goddess witch was showing her evil side. He needed to save his ship, then head to Illumahrah again like a maddened spirit.

After turning his dark cloak to show its green side, he glamoured the points of his ears away, then magicked his horns so they were invisible. With the eye patch he kept in the cloak's interior pocket and a glamoured beard, the look was complete. The magic exhausted him more than usual, an effect of his anxiety level. Recovering from this journey was going to require an incredible amount of fine chocolate, expensive wine, beautiful companions, and quite possibly, a new cloak. Werian sighed, grinning, his natural optimism winning out as he imagined Little John safely far away. Being a swashbuckling fae prince with a secret identity was truly exhausting in the best of ways.

CHAPTER 7

RHIANNE

Of course, sleep mostly evaded Rhianne. Though Nor and the other women who lived and worked the castle grounds kindly welcomed her in and gave her a tidy cot, dreams teased her, just out of grasp. Not only was she sleeping in a castle born of magic, a place legends claimed had a mind of its own, she was still reeling from the wolf attack, the witch's refusal to reveal Rhianne's match, and meeting a fae face-to-face.

Rhianne pulled the blanket up to her chin. The other women's light snores and deep breathing filled the room. To aid her healing, she needed a good rest, and being awake wouldn't solve any problems. The witch slept at night like the others, so Nor had said, and Werian had taken his leave. Any decisions she might make about her future had to wait. It wasn't as if she could read the loom herself and see the match that had angered the witch beyond reason. Only the witch could See.

But it wouldn't hurt to simply look at the loom. Would it?

Stomach churning, she sat up.

If the witch caught her snooping around though...

She lay down again, forcing her eyes shut and listening to the concert of snoring. There was no point in sneaking around that magical loom just to see nothing and then have the witch catch her and throw her out with no further mention of a match at all.

Starlight drifted through the small, high windows that ran along the front wall of the room. The shadow of a cloud blackened the first window for a moment before the stars glittered again.

The steady crunch of shoes on leaves trickled from outside the building.

Rhianne clutched her blanket as a torch's light brightened the window, blotting out the sky. She held her breath to listen. Whoever it was kept on, past the servants' quarters and farther into the courtyard. A thief? Another castle worker?

Sliding out of bed, she moved quickly. She tugged her shoes over her recently mended stockings, then pulled her dress over her shift, lacing the front with shaking fingers.

If it were a thief or a brigand, she would need a weapon. She didn't want to wake the castle if it were nothing. She'd look first, armed and prepared.

Seeing nothing sharper than a sewing needle on the room's two tables, she dumped her tallow candle from its pig-iron base. The candle holder would serve well enough. Hopefully.

The door scraped the threshold as she opened it far enough to slip through.

Firelight from the bobbing torch grabbed her attention. Torchlight danced over the witch's ivy-green hair and lit the straw-lined path. An owl called to another beyond the castle's courtyard wall, and Rhianne inhaled, hoping to catch the scent of the fae but smelling only banked fires, goats in the nearby barn, and the autumn leaves.

Wherever the witch was going, she was in a hurry. Where had she been?

It wasn't wise to follow a witch into her own castle. It wasn't wise to follow a witch at all. But this witch had a secret, and that secret involved Rhianne.

As the firelight vanished behind the great wooden door, Rhianne's practical nature crumbled to dust. Without another thought, she headed toward the castle, trailing the witch like a shadow.

RHIANNE HAD TO WONDER HOW LONG THE WITCH MIGHT keep the truth of her match a secret. How long would she be here, so far away from home? To what end? Werian seemed like a dream, a dream she so wanted to chase, but what if she were being foolish? What if adventure didn't lay in her stars?

Grasping the candlestick in case the witch flew into another wild rage, Rhianne pressed her lips tight to keep from calling out. Before she announced her presence, she wanted to see what the witch was doing. Perhaps she would sit at her loom and Rhianne could glean some information from the witch's constant muttering. If the witch mentioned the match, then Rhianne could locate the man herself by questioning the villagers who lived near the wood. She could watch him and decide if he deserved her and if he was willing. Then she would decide whether or not to take Werian up on his offer.

Obviously, the chance to ride alongside a fae prince was more interesting and attractive than anything she could imagine. But if taking that adventure ruined her chance at a lifelong, supportive relationship, she'd have to think twice.

The witch pushed into the room where they had eaten their onion soup. Rhianne kept her distance, sliding from shadow to shadow before ducking into a corner. Muttering, the witch passed the water basin beside the front door and removed a small item from a shelf. Pausing, her back to Rhianne, the witch lifted her chin.

"Who is there? Nor? Isuelt? Margaret?" The witch took three steps closer to the cauldron, closer to Rhianne. "Ancient witches?" The witch's voice sounded like two sheets of parchment rubbing. "Do I need to pay my due? I had thought my equinox sacrifice was enough. Are you not pleased with me?"

What ancient witches? Her due? Rhianne held her breath and hugged herself, trying to keep her cacophonous heartbeat from waking the entire world. It was strange, unsettling, to hear the powerful witch use such submissive tones.

"Ach." The witch tucked the small item from the shelf into the front of her dress and waved a hand dismissively, obviously deciding there was nothing to fret about. She walked across the room, then into the great hall, where the loom waited.

Rhianne tiptoed through the starlit kitchen, past the cauldron that still smelled of onions despite being magically washed clean. At the entrance to the great hall, she concealed herself behind the wide wood of the door framing. She pressed her nose against the grain and kept her arm in tight beside her, allowing just one eye and half her face to be exposed. Every breath sounded like a hunter's horn as she tried to keep quiet.

The witch didn't bother to sit in her willow-branch chair. She stood at the loom and stared into its sparkling woolen weave, shuttle in hand. The first faint light of dawn slipped over her gnarled fingers. "Show me another match for the girl," she muttered. "She cannot have him. The queen would never allow it."

Rhianne's heart jumped over two beats and skittered to a stop. The witch had to be talking about her.

The witch thrust the shuttle between the threads. Painted by the windows' colors of autumn sky, poppy red, oak leaf, and iris, starlight sailed on unseen magic to drift over the loom's black frame.

"The Queen in the Hill would drive me into the underworld for it! Please, show me another match. She's not so bad, this one. But she is not for him, and he is not for her." The witch's head tilted as the vision in the wool showed itself. "It cannot be." She threw the shuttle, and it clattered to the flagstones. Slamming her hands into the base of the loom's frame, she shouted, "I refuse it!"

The ground shook in earnest this time, and the tremor could not be reasoned away. Plumes of dust unfurled from the chamber's walls and down from the rough-hewn beams. Beside the loom, a crack slithered like a great snake through the flagstones. Another jagged line opened under a tapestry and followed the mortar all the way to the chamber's back door. The room smelled like sage and lightning, like magic raising its head to the wind.

Rhianne forgot to hide, fear grabbing her throat with icicle fingers. She couldn't die now, not when her life was just getting started.

"Mistress witch!" she called out, though the witch's fierce expression gave no comfort against this wild quaking of the ground. "How can I help?"

Eyebrows bunched, the witch reeled. "Cobbler girl! What are you doing here?" The skin around her mouth paled to a sickly white, and a vein in her temple throbbed.

Rhianne held her candlestick aloft between them.

A cracking broke her focus on the witch. Both turned to the directional windows.

The blue glass shattered. Shrieking, the witch crouched as if something might reach through that window and grab her. Rhianne gripped the doorframe and coughed dust from her lungs as the castle continued to tremble. The air snapped with electricity like the sky before a storm. One emotion came to mind. Rage.

The castle was angry.

Cracks snaked down the red and green windows, the glass clicking like an asp about to spring. The dark lavender window blasted into the room and launched spears of itself at the witch, who shouted and dropped to her knees to hide near her chair.

Rhianne let the candlestick fall and ran to the woman,

dragging her toward another door, one that appeared to lead to the barn. "We must leave, or we'll be crushed! We have to alert the others!"

Between the loom and the door, the witch jerked upright and shoved Rhianne, whose shoes slid on the glass as she let out a scream. Rhianne's back slammed into the wall, but she managed to remain standing.

"This is all your fault!" The witch's willow-branch wand flew from the kitchen and snapped into her waiting palm. "I was going to match him to a high lady and earn the queen's favor and live amongst the fae and their spirit agate for eternity!"

Thoughts swirled through Rhianne's head. What did her match have to do with the witch gaining a favored place in the Fae Court? And would that mean the witch would become immortal? Rhianne didn't know very much about spirit agate and the fae. What could she say to calm the witch's madness?

"You have ruined it all with your low birth," the witch spat. "And your reckless bravery, and now, now you will die." She pointed the wand at Rhianne's forehead. "A bane, a bane, unmake, undo. A bane, a bane, from this life, I banish you!"

Light exploded from the wand in a ball of obsidian smoke and ivory light. The magic rushed toward Rhianne. She turned to flee, managed two steps, but then an unseen force gripped every muscle, tendon, and bone, stilled her heart, her lungs. Only her eyes could move as she floated, strands of hair around her face like rays of light and her raised foot trapped mid-stride.

Three voices trickled through her ears. They spoke as one. "This Matchweaver has wronged her craft."

Rhianne tried to turn her head, but the strange magic held her in place. Who was speaking? They sounded like old men, their voices a mix of reedy, powerful, and wise.

"We entrust the castle to your keeping," they said. "You must bring forth the next Matchweaver."

Thrashing from one question to another, Rhianne's mind reeled. Why? How? She was no witch. She knew little of witches at all. Still frozen in time, cold fear began to outstrip her feral survival instincts, and her mind worked out the possibilities.

Did she have a choice?

The castle's shaking ceased, and she collapsed, released from the spell. In a rush that made her lightheaded, Rhianne's breath and heartbeat returned to normal.

The witch's wails began anew.

Rhianne's first thought was Nor. She looked in the direction of the barn and the sleeping quarters, searching for signs of damage created by the quaking ground. The witch stood slowly.

Shaking, Rhianne prayed that Nor and the rest of the women were all right. She tried to call out to them even as the witch closed the distance between them, but Rhianne's throat burned. She'd nearly screamed herself hoarse. Only the castle's magic could've kept the other women from hearing all the commotion, further proving the fact that Rhianne was meant to solve this on her own.

CHAPTER 8
WERIAN

Moon carried Werian at a quick gallop down the black cobblestones of the main road that slithered through the wind-and-salt-battered city of the Sea's Claw. The buildings sloped as they rose, nearly touching rooftops, leaning on one another like old men gathered to gossip.

Werian gasped. A massive, jade-colored dragon hovered above the harbor where hundreds of ships bobbed. Including his.

"Go!" he shouted to Moon, and the horse responded, speeding like only a mount fed by fae healing magic could.

Drunkards stumbled from the Owl and Leaf, their pipe smoke snaking into the air and their laughs grating on the ears.

"Move, fools!" Werian eased Moon around the men and women, who called out curses on his head.

Where were Jewel, Filip, and Aury? The skies held only

that single dragon. The winged creature shook its crystal-spiked head like something below in the harbor pained it.

The road stopped at the docks, and Werian launched off of Moon to run down the third dock until he stood aboard his dark, fast-as-a-demon ship, *Nucklavee*. It wasn't a large vessel, but it had plenty of space for the merry band's short trips down the coastline and to Khem. The sails were tied neatly and the deck scrubbed to shining. He tugged the hood of his green cloak over his head.

"John!" Where was everyone?

A roar sounded above. The jade dragon focused on the *Nucklavee's* crow's nest, wings hammering the air and bending the dockside pines with forced wind.

"What in the name of Arcturus and his twin sons is up there?" Eyeing the crow's nest, he began to climb the mast. "It's not like I really wanted to live past this day," he grumbled, knowing full well this was the most imbecilic move he'd ever made. At least the dragon hadn't fired on him yet.

Yet.

With the beating wings of a death beast not a stone's throw from his glamour-hidden horns, Werian leapt deftly into the crow's nest only to find an open sack of bright gold coins.

Shouting on the docks turned his head. Little John waved and ran toward the ship, the rest of the crew trailing his massive form. They were white-faced, and little did Werian blame them. If the dragon didn't kill them, he would.

"Gold in the crow's nest? Really? That's your fantastic hiding spot for the year's take?" He twisted the sack shut, hefted the bundle, climbed out of the nest, and then down the mast. If there was one thing that would pull a dragon from the highest clouds, it was gold. Sure, they were a rare sight, but they enjoyed feasting on seals and were seen more here than anywhere in Lore.

The dragon roared and blew fire.

Heat seared the tips of Werian's invisible horns, and he hissed in pain. "Aury and Filip," he mumbled, "now would be a great time to show up." Only Filip seemed able to communicate with dragons. The elven prince had claimed he was no mage, indeed that no elves were, but he possessed a capability that certainly seemed like magic. He could deny it all he wanted, but the people of Lore had deemed him a mage, and so he was.

The bag of gold was heavy in Werian's grip. There was no use fighting the outcome. The gold had to go into the sea, or the dragon would blaze the entire harbor. Werian had no desire to become a puddle of melted fae on the deck of his sleek pirate ship.

With a mighty toss, he heaved the sack of coins into the white-capped waves. While the crew halted at the gangplank of the *Nucklavee*, the dragon shot toward the splash of the gold into the water. Drawing up short, the dragon gave up and pulled itself toward the stars on straining wings, tendons taut and eyes shining as it roared with rage and disappointment. Dragons loathed sea water, almost as if the very liquid could curse them into some horrific death.

Exhaling in relief, Werian started to ask John and the others what had been going on in their heads when they stashed the take in the nest, but the dragon shrieked and dove straight at the ship.

The creature's mouth opened wide, and Werian's fae eyes saw every jagged tooth clearly, the veins in the dragon's thin, forked tongue, the spark of fire rising in its throat. The scent of charred wood and lemon filled the air —a scent particular to dragons.

Werian froze.

If he could somehow strike that sensitive tongue, he had a chance. He unsheathed the ruby encrusted dagger he kept on his belt. Any hesitation, and he'd be a dragon's midnight morsel.

He threw the knife.

Silver as starlight and red as the dragon's eyes, the blade shot toward the beast as Werian braced himself for death. A shriek pealed from the dragon's mouth as the blade caught the tip of the creature's tongue. A line of blood appeared at Werian's feet, then the dragon was flying high, wheeling and yowling in pain.

The beast disappeared into the darkness. They would live another day.

Werian grimaced, wishing he hadn't been forced to hurt the majestic being. No doubt the creatures were nearly as intelligent as fae. If only Filip the elven mage had been here...

Little John and the crew boarded the ship, cheering and shouting his false name. John knew Werian's true identity. The others did not, and that information was kept from them for their own safety as well as Werian's. If the king ever managed to capture any of the crew, the less they were involved in the deception, the better it would go for them.

"Shadowhood!"

"Captain 'Hood!"

John threw a beefy arm around Werian's neck and pulled him in for a quick hug. Werian fought a grin and shoved him away.

"Ah, now," Werian said, adjusting his eye patch, the most dashing part of his invented disguise. "We're fine, aren't we? I must know why you chose to flash our take to the skies."

John shrugged, looking much like a bear. He rubbed the scar that ran down the left side of his face and glanced at Werian. "The tax men surprised us. We had no time to think it out. And who could guess a dragon would be nearby?"

"And why was no one aboard, keeping watch?"

They all looked sheepish then, Eamon scratching his yellow beard and looking everywhere but at Werian. The sailor was a liar and would steal the boots off a man not yet cold in his grave, but with a little direction, Eamon had shown signs of growing at least a pirate-style moral compass. He was the most fun to tease because he took himself far more seriously than anyone ever should.

"Spill it, Eamon," Werian snapped.

Eamon exhaled and spread his arms wide. "They had the dancing girls up at the Owl and Leaf. You know we can't miss them. It's only once a year!"

The other men nodded solemnly.

"I hope you got an eyeful but kept your coin in your pocket, because now we have precious little to spread around." Werian crossed his arms as they all looked to the sea where he'd tossed the sack. "Well, if I'm going to lose a fortune in one day, it had better be an amazing night. Dragon fight, check. Let's go see if the dancing ladies have any pep left in their step."

"Aye!" Little John led the way off the ship and into the city proper, Eamon singing a terrible song behind him.

Werian smiled at his merry band of agate thieves, wishing he were as excited at the prospect of silk-wrapped lovelies spinning and smiling at a warm tavern. But all he could think about was how many shades of rust and root he'd seen in brave Rhianne's flashing eyes.

ANOTHER DRAGON LANDED NEAR THE DOCKS AS DAWN gilded the harbor's ragtag fleet of cogs, knarrs, caravals, and longships, startling the horses housed in the waterside stables. Werian raised a hand in greeting as Princess Aurora —Aury—and Prince Filip jumped from their dragon friend's sparsely spiked back. A crowd of merchants, dirty-cheeked children, and a host of mangy curs gathered to watch. Werian would have to be careful to keep his voice down and his hood up. Glamour or not, the city folk would wonder indeed why the princess of Lore and her prince were visiting a lowly trader. Thankfully, they'd not dressed in full regal attire. Aury wore her midnight blue Darkfleot tunic, her runed staff strapped to her back. In a thin tunic and incredibly dull trousers and boots, Filip looked as though he had just rolled out of bed. But their mode of transportation was less than subtle. He was grateful they'd come so quickly though. They must have feared the worst.

The dragon, Jewel, lowered herself into a ball on the

dockside as if she were a massive, blue-scaled cat. She promptly began snoring, making the children laugh.

Werian fought a yawn and stretched his arms, wishing he'd slept in a bed of goose down rather than the rickety straw nightmare at the Owl and Leaf. He'd stayed up late negotiating with his trade contact before sleeping for a few hours. With one last check on the crew and the ship, Werian was ready for his return to the Forest of Illumahrah and the witch, to tempt the truth from the crone and make certain Rhianne was safe from harm.

"Hello, Cousin!" Aury whispered, nodding instead of hugging him because of the crowd, certainly. The sea breeze whipped her long, silver hair around her face. She pushed it back and smiled.

"You look well handled, lovely one." He gave her a wink, and she feigned an angry glare.

"Mind your own business, Werian," she said, her cheeks flushing pink. "That disguise of yours is incredibly convincing. Do you glamour that beard?"

"I do," he said.

"I'd consider keeping it." Aury studied his face, her blue eyes narrowed in concentration. "It becomes you."

"I'm not sure you understand how disguises work. If Werian has the same beard as Shadowhood..."

She poked his ribs. "You could come up with a reason. The ladies would like it."

"I'm not struggling to find lovers, my darling cousin."

Aury waved her hands. "All right. I don't want to know. Forget I asked."

Werian fought a grin.

Filip gave a shallow bow, and the sun glinted off the

mountain-style braids woven tightly above the shaved sides of his head. "Greetings." Aury's gaze drank the man in.

Werian bowed in return, warmth filling his chest. "I see you two are managing to suffer through your arranged marriage." The pair appeared pleased as dragons in gold to be in one another's company. "You're both so selfless. Giving up your freedom. All for crown and country, hmm?"

Filip grinned and rubbed the back of his neck, his eyebrow twitching. "It's a maddening challenge."

Aury gasped and smacked his chest. "I'll show you mad."

Filip held up his war-scarred hands as if in surrender, his eyes flashing with mirth.

Aury faced Werian as they boarded the ship. "I heard you chased the dragon off yourself. Did you truly throw your best dagger and pierce its tongue?"

"When one doesn't have fighting magic or dragons as allies," Werian said, "one must resort to steel and the brilliant courage of the ancient heroes."

Aury crossed her arms. "It seems that package doesn't come with a supply of humility."

"Humility is overrated." Werian leaned against the mast and brushed a stray seagull feather from his green cloak.

"I'm just surprised you were willing to part with that ruby-encrusted blade."

"Eamon is diving for it as we speak. Eamon!"

A splash sounded beyond the ship, and Eamon's bright voice carried over the call of gulls and the bump of the boats against the docks. "Not found it yet, Captain Hood! But I will. I swear on my honor!"

Werian sighed and regarded Aury. "Well, that dagger's

lost for good, then. A shame." He gave Aury a kiss on the cheek, then gripped Filip's shoulder and squeezed it. "I wish I could stay and take you around the city. The chandler here crafts a magnificent lavender candle that smells like hope divine, but I must go."

"Where to?" Aury trailed him off the ship.

Little John came tromping down the dock with a new rope looped over a shoulder.

"John," Werian said. "Will you chase this crowd off?"

"Give them a seven?" John's bushy eyebrows lifted.

"No. Too early for that. I think a three is in order."

John barked a laugh. "All right, Captain." He threw the rope aboard, then swung around to face the gathered city folk. "Eh, Beorn!"

Beorn was coming up behind the crowd, his head easily visible over the jeweler and his rosy-faced wife. "Aye, John?"

"Halig's honey shortbread is half price this morning! Get me two loaves, would you?"

The crowd murmured, shifting their weight, until the children shouted, "Shortbread!" They ran off, the rest of the folk following nearly as quick on their feet.

"I believe I feel insulted," Aury said.

"No," Werian explained, "Halig's bakery is the afterlife you dream of but could never deserve. No mere mortal could possibly compete. Nor any dragons."

Jewel's blue head rose, and she snorted, obviously affronted.

Filip grinned and shook his head.

"You truly can hear her thoughts, can't you, elven mage?" Werian studied the man's quick, gray eyes and the points of his ears, far sharper than his own.

"She thinks these are your people and that you and they value food more than the sight of one as rare as she," Filip said.

"You are the jewel your prince has deemed you. No offense intended," Werian said, pulling his hood farther over his eyes so none could see him clearly as they walked on.

Aury and Filip followed him to the end of the dock and bid him farewell.

"I'd offer Jewel's conveyance, if you wish it," Filip offered.

"No. Moon would be most affronted if I left him with this lot."

Little John was removing the old rope that held the boat to the docking. He must have heard Werian, because he made a very rude gesture with his hand, too quick for most to see.

Werian saluted John, then took Moon's reins from the stable hand and mounted up. "I ride for the witch's castle. I fear she has another foul plan in mind and it has to do with me."

Aury's neck reddened, and she pulled her staff from its place on her baldric. "I'm coming with you."

"No, no, no. You've done too much for this spoiled... fellow already." He'd nearly mentioned his position, and the stable hand was not two steps away. "I'll send word if I need your aid. She's much diminished since you cut her down. I can handle her."

With one last wave, he and Moon sped into the morning, the wind in their faces and the growl of thunder above.

CHAPTER 9

RHIANNE

Looming over Rhianne, the witch stood—too still, too quiet. Her hair was bright as any emerald, but wild strands had escaped the coiled braid on top to hang over her ears and the lines of her forehead. The rising sun pierced the broken windows behind her and cast her shadow over a basket of woven blankets and the Mageloom.

"What have you done?" the witch whispered, her gaze skirting from Rhianne to the loom. The willow-branch wand shook in her fingers. She looked like a crazed, injured animal.

Chills dragged down Rhianne's back. She held up her hands, fingers splayed, desperate to keep the woman calm. For all she knew, the witch still had power, and it didn't look like she was in the mood to discuss things rationally. "Please. I didn't mean to do anything. I don't even know what is happening. There were voices in my ears, and they stopped my heart. I don't—"

The witch's wand twitched in her grip. "You are not fae-blooded. You should not be fae-matched. To think of *you* with Prince Werian." She sucked a breath through her teeth.

The words clicked into place. Prince Werian. The Prince of the Agate Court, son to the Queen in the Hill. And he was Rhianne's match. No wonder the witch wanted Rhianne dead. With Rhianne gone, the Mageloom might show the witch a high-born match for Prince Werian, and then the Fae Queen would shower the witch with favor and, if the stories were true, immortality. It all made sense.

The room tilted, and Rhianne widened her stance to keep from toppling.

Drawing an invisible circle over her head, the witch spoke in a low and rasping voice. "I will right this wrong. I will have my revenge on you, Rhianne of Tyreh. Mark me! You may have stolen the castle witches' power, but I still have mine. You are no true witch."

The air around the Matchweaver's bright hair snapped like a clap of thunder. "Bind it, seal it. Lock the loom. My soul, their souls, they chose their doom."

Wind lashed out at the loom, and the black frame shuddered. Flames erupted from the woolen threads.

Sweating, tears burning her eyes, Rhianne shouted for help and ran at the loom. She grabbed one of the woven blankets, thinking to suffocate the flames. Without this loom, love would disappear from the kingdom. No one knew what that outcome would look like in reality, but every story deemed it as truth, and she had no desire to see that horrible fate come to fruition in any imaginable form.

The blanket unrolled like a bird's wing as she threw it across the fire.

The floor of the great hall shuddered. The flagstones heaved and thrust her away from the loom. She stumbled backward. The blanket she'd thrown slid from the black frame. The fire had vanished, and the magical apparatus remained intact and whole, not a single flame flickering over the rainbow of woolen yarn.

The Matchweaver's body glittered like starlight, the intensity increasing moment by moment, now almost too bright to look at. The crone gasped, then hooted as if in victory. Her form shimmered, a thousand colors reflected in the bits that shaped her limbs, head, torso. Then the glittering pieces drew into a cloud-like shape, drifted into the rafters, then out of the broken window.

"You've unleashed me now..." The Matchweaver's voice echoed and buzzed in Rhianne's ears, foul laughter following the menacing words until all fell silent.

Nothing of the old witch remained, not even her willow wand or chair of braided branches.

Sweat bloomed across Rhianne's back and she wiped her damp forehead. What now? The ancient witches never should have put the castle in her hands. Madness! The witch had said Rhianne had stolen the castle's magic, but she felt nothing in her veins, no spark, no—

A new wand shimmered into existence at her feet.

It was not willow, but made of light, reddish rowan, straight and carved with intertwining circles. Her fingers itched to pick it up, and so she did. The moment the wand touched her flesh, pleasant shivers danced over her palms.

Then a heavy force like an unseen wave rushed through her chest, stole her breath, and bathed her face in heat.

The ancient witches spoke. "With this wand, you carry our power." Their voices grew together to become one, echoing and distant. "Raise the next Matchweaver. Hurry! The former will take your life."

Cold speared her heart. "Won't your magic protect me? This was your idea, not mine. I don't mean to be ungrateful, but..." Clutching the wand, the desperation to understand, to know more, flooded her mind. "How do I find another witch? How long do I have?"

Only the chirping of birds filled her ears. She swallowed. Impossible. The wand warmed her hand like a patch of sunlight on the grass, and she gripped it tightly, taking comfort from its surprising heft.

She stared into the Mageloom, trying to see something, a sign, a message... Time seemed to stop. The birds' song froze on one note. None of the women came to see what was happening. The dust in the sunlight refused to spin. She touched the loom, and a drumming pounded through her bones. But there was nothing to see in the magicked yarn. The dust danced again in the air, and the birds went on with their singing. The sun had lowered in the window as if time had only frozen here on the castle grounds while it continued on outside the boundaries. This was definitely magical. Time had flowed backward, around—in some new way she had never experienced.

How much time had she already wasted? She swallowed, panic rising. Had it been hours, days?

A scuffing sound told her someone had come in

through the kitchen door. A heaviness suffused her, and her palms grew damp. She didn't want to turn around, to admit the truth of what had happened and how unfit she was for the quest set upon her. She would look like the greatest fool, but it did no good to deny it.

Heart weighted, she pivoted to see Werian. Prince Werian.

"Well met, fellow warrior," he said.

A thudding permeated the air. Was the castle shaking again? No, it was her own pulse, hammering at her ears. He appeared exactly as striking as he'd been last night. Perhaps more so, because the sun's golden rays highlighted the plum and ebony hues of his hair and horns. His eyes were clearly not human—the irises took up too much of the eye, and his lashes were far thicker than any human man's. She wanted to go on drinking in his image for as long as was polite. Maybe longer.

Crossing one pointed boot over the other, he gave her a smile and cocked an eyebrow. A tingling sensation spread down her stomach. "Well, you seem to have had a busy day." His accent added length to his *U*.

Her breaths came far too quickly, and the room seemed hazy. It'd all been too much. She needed to sit down and think. "This isn't good. It's trouble. And I don't have any idea what to do with it."

He took a step closer, one hand still on the doorframe where she had hidden herself from the witch so recently. It felt like a lifetime ago. "I've always been attracted to trouble."

A nervous laugh bubbled from her throat, and she

shook her head. "I wanted adventure, but this, this is beyond...anything." How could she tell him she was his match? Would he even believe her? Goddess Vahly bless her, she could not imagine taking his hand, let alone—

"Perhaps you should sit." He procured a chair from the kitchen in two blinks of an eye.

Thanking him, Rhianne settled and began to tell him the tale about the witch's anger with her match, though she kept the details to herself. He listened, his eyebrows knitted in concern as she described the spell, the ancient witches' voices, and the wand. Her courage wavered when it was past time to tell him whom she was meant to marry.

Hitched up against the loom, he crossed his arms, his face narrowed in concentration. "What could possibly be so horrible about your match? Do you know the man?"

A tickle attacked her throat, and she coughed, face on fire. What if he denied her? But she had to tell him. She took a breath and met his otherworldly gaze.

"You, Prince Werian, are my match." The wand nearly fell from her grasp, but she caught it with shaking fingers.

His features relaxed, and he dropped to one knee. "I knew it."

Her chest tightened. She gripped the wand and the chair to keep from tumbling right over at his feet. "You did?"

Lifting that eyebrow of his again, he nodded at her unbroken hand. She lifted her palm to him. His mouth descended onto her wrist, soft lips pressing a kiss over her frantic pulse point. The heat of his breath and the sight of his hair shifting around his bowed and horned head stole every possible response from her mouth. He was so lovely. So different.

Looking up, his wide eyes searched her face as if she were a map that told of great treasures. It was an expression she had never thought would be directed at her. Her heart shivered, and her fingers curled around his warm and calloused palms.

"If you'll take the time to know me," he said, "I would be pleased with this match. I've seen you. In my dreams. Astride a dappled mare and fighting at my side."

Her mouth popped open as she recalled her own dreams. "I have seen you too. With that beetle-black sword of yours and a white stallion."

His smile was brighter and warmer than sunlight. "I must admit, when you showed up here, I wondered if I might be losing my mind."

Together, they stood. She didn't want to take him into her arms yet. Not until they knew one another more. But the temptation was there, and so she kept a few inches between them.

He bowed his head a fraction as if to acknowledge the boundary she'd drawn. "How do you wish to begin this quest to find the next Matchweaver?"

An idea scurried through her head. If she had magic now, there were those she might see set straight. For the good of everyone, of course. "I want to try something. Would you like to come along?"

His fingers brushed hers, and a sizzling heat hurried over her body. "I will go with you anywhere. I am yours," he whispered reverently, his gaze half-lidded, "for as long as you wish it."

Throat going dry, she tried to swallow. His lips were so close. The scent he carried, so much like Naroniti spices, haunting and musky against her senses. Before she could fall into his arms, she whirled and led him away.

It was time for a little reckoning.

CHAPTER 10
WERIAN

At the back door of the keep, Werian bowed as Rhianne left to speak with Nor. He watched Rhianne walk across the leaf-strewn courtyard, and excitement warmed him like a fine wine. Her small fingers gripped her new wand, her pinky held up just slightly. Hips swaying gently as she went, her feet lightly crossing the grounds... He marveled at her grace. Despite her simple clothing, she looked more noble fae than human cobbler.

And the way she rose to this wild challenge? A smile stretched his lips. Amazing. This was unprecedented, the Source giving a wand to a non-witch, the magical instrument simply appearing at her feet. So strange! He laughed, delighted by the rarity of it.

The sun glazed her chestnut tresses, and he longed to run his hands through that hair, to tug it lightly and pull her close. What would she enjoy? A soft kiss? A nip on the delicate lobe of her ear? A shiver of desire rushed across his skin, and he shifted his weight. There would be time enough for that.

At the castle's stables, he saddled Moon, then found a fine mare for Rhianne. The beast was dappled like the one in his dreams. He wished he had a sword or dagger to give to Rhianne as well, but perhaps that could be a wedding gift if all went well. First, he had to tell her all about his secret identity.

Perhaps Aury's vision of him sailing with a brunette had been the sight of Rhianne and him aiming to search for the next Matchweaver in Khem? It was as good a plan as any, and it would be telling to see how she interacted with the crew. He wondered what kind of pirate this match of his might make.

Rhianne would need a disguise and a false name to shield her from the past pirating in which he and the crew had participated. He wouldn't tell the crew who or what she was. Well, except for Little John. He'd tell Little John everything.

An eerie, quiet howling sounded in Werian's ears. He spun to see if the stable boy had heard the noise, but the lad kept on cleaning out the shoes on a piebald two stalls down.

"Take her to the island," three voices said in unison. "She will find truth at the well."

"Boy! Did you hear that?" Werian called out, his hand hovering over the buckle on the dappled mare's girth.

"My lord?" The boy blinked at him.

"When the raven cries thrice," the voices moaned. "Love will die, and death will take us all."

Werian swallowed, suddenly cold. "What well?" he whispered, feeling completely mad.

There was no answer except the quiet howling.

"Boy, you must ride the fastest pony here that you can handle. You must take a message to the ship of Captain Shadowhood at the Sea's Claw. Ask around. You will find it in the harbor easily enough. Leave the message with his first mate, John, if you must."

Werian took a slip of parchment and a sharpened bit of charcoal from the small bag on his belt. He wrote a note to John telling him to ready the ship for sailing to Khem, then handed the folded missive to the boy.

"This charcoal holds a curse," Werian lied. The boy flinched but kept hold of the parchment. "If you read this note," Werian said, "your stones will fall right off your body before you reach full manhood. Now, go!"

The boy went white but raced to the nearest pony.

Werian took the reins of Moon and the dappled mare and hurried to find Rhianne. This day was half over. How long would they have to figure this out? The trip to Khem would take at least a day on its own. He set his jaw. If the task the ancients had set upon them was impossible, so be it. But if it could be done, he and Rhianne would accomplish it, for who could be more worthy of such a quest than Shadowhood and his lady?

CHAPTER 11

RHIANNE

After regaling Nor and the other women who worked at the castle with all the details of the early morning, Rhianne joined Werian to ride through the wood, retracing the journey she'd had on foot the night of Mabon. The wild violets, bright orange trumpet vines, and oak saplings bowed to Werian as they progressed—green servants to his fae power.

Even though she had an impossible task set on her by the ancient witches, Rhianne's cheeks hurt from grinning.

"I hate to ruin that smile, but I have news," Werian said, glancing over his shoulder.

He had removed his cloak, rolled it, and tied it to his saddle. Her gaze traveled from his broad shoulders down his back. The lines and slopes of well-shaped muscles showed beneath his shirt, and his waist tapered into his wide belt. He was such a fine-looking prince. It was impossible to believe he was fated to be hers. Still turned in his saddle, he looked her in the eye.

She cleared her throat, trying to relieve its sudden dryness. "Go on," she said, petting Storm's neck. The mare nickered happily. "I can see from your face it's nothing good, and things like that are best met and dealt with as quickly as possible."

He told of being two people, one of whom stole agate from his court to sell in order to irritate his mother and help the poor folk in the eastern province. Then he explained his disguise and asked if she would be amenable to wearing one as well.

The idea excited her. "Of course. I want straight black hair and golden eyes. Maybe you could give me a scar over my cheek to further hide my identity? I will take the name..." Hmm. What was a good pirate woman's name?

"Berthe?" Werian suggested, the lift of his right eyebrow telling her he was joking. "Allonfonsa Alfreda Althelfred?"

She laughed. "That's more name than anyone could ever need. How about Merewyn? I once heard a story about a Merewyn who had powerful magic and a prince at her side."

He pulled Moon back so that he rode beside her. "That is a new one to me, but I like it. Merewyn it is," he said. "Merewyn the Feared."

"Merewyn of the Bones."

His head tilted back, and the sunlight through the trees painted a pattern over his features. "Ooo la, I like that one. Very dark. But there is more to tell you, and it's not as pleasant. The ancient witches spoke to me."

She gripped the reins so tightly that the leather bit into her skin.

"They told me that we have until the raven cries three times to visit a well in Khem. If we fail to raise the new Matchweaver by then, love will die and death will take us all."

"The ancients spoke to you?" A raven calling? That could happen in one afternoon! "So they didn't offer a proper timeline?" Rhianne shook her head. How was one supposed to plan without an exact measure of days?

"Personally," Werian said, placing a hand over his heart, "I would have liked something a bit more encouraging. A *you can do this, young lovers!* Or maybe even a *We have instilled the power in yon lovely cobbler to accomplish it, so fret not!*"

"How long does it take for your ship to sail to Khem?"

"I sent word to my men to prepare. Once we've taken care of your business here, we can ride hard and sail to Khem. Depending on the wind, it takes a day, maybe a day and a half. That's the best I can do."

"It will have to be enough."

When they reached her village of Tyreh, the villagers gawked, dropping baskets and shooing small children away as she rode down the main thoroughfare with her wand at the ready and Werian riding at her side. Her heart was light and her anger blazing. But she had to bank that fire for a moment and see her uncle.

Inside the shop, amid the smells of hide and pipe smoke, Uncle Cane sat at his workbench and hummed in that distracted way he had. His mind was sharp, and he was a master cobbler—she was proud of him. But he'd never been overly involved in her life. No embraces or questions about the day.

The sun from the one window cascaded over cut strips

of leather, his new awl, and the hammer he preferred for smaller projects.

"Good afternoon, Uncle." She had asked Werian to remain outside. No need to frighten the old man.

Starting, he clasped his hammer to his chest. "Oh, it's you. I had thought you'd be longer at the witch's castle. Did you approve of your match?"

"It's complicated. But I want you to know I'm happy, and I'll be gone for a long while."

He was already back to his project, punching holes in the leather. "Of course, dear. Whatever you want. I have plenty of help here, so feel free to move on. But come back to visit time and again, if you please. I would hate to go forever without seeing my brother's daughter."

His words pinched her—a familiar pain—and she pursed her lips. He hadn't even noticed the change in her or the fact that she held a wand. Shrugging, she left the workshop for the last time. By goddess Vahly's sacred dice, she'd not waste time with this town any longer.

"Everything well?" Werian asked as they started down the road on foot, their horses following.

In front of the tavern, two bay geldings snuffed a pile of alfalfa, unaware of the forthcoming drama.

"Same as it always was," she said. "It's fine. He won't miss me. He's an odd sort, my uncle. I need to tell you about a man we're about to meet." She informed him that Odo had been the one to hurt her first in the forest, before the scar wolf's attack, and that she had to have her reckoning before they left. Odo couldn't be allowed to treat anyone else the way he'd treated her.

Werian grew very quiet, his eyes narrowed. They

walked without talking, letting the wind roll over their shoulders. Werian's particular scent comforted her despite the situation or maybe because of it. She knew, somehow, that he was completely on her side.

Hushed gossip stirred around the village.

"He is a fae!"

"Don't look him in the eye. He'll bewitch you. Caught that stupid girl already, you can see that. He'll chew her up and spit her out before the day's gone."

"Always hated that left-handed woman. What's she here for now? And with one of those?"

"Shut it! She has a wand. Look!"

The gossip turned to awed silence as the villagers pushed their faces into their windows and doorways to peek at the downtrodden girl who had become a witch with a fae at her side.

At the end of the lane, Odo's brewhouse was quiet.

It would not be so for long.

Holding her wand, Rhianne called out, "Odo!"

A few doves exploded into flight, dashing away from their stone wall near the twelve-foot-high cauldron where Odo boiled his ale. The wheelwright peeked through his window across the way. The baker's children pointed from their mother's stall.

"What is the cause of all this noise?" Odo stomped out of his brewhouse, wiping his meaty hands on a stained cloth. He raised his face, then drew up short. Color drained from his ruddy cheeks as he took in both Werian and Rhianne's wand, poised to strike. Then he seemed to gather himself, tucking his cloth into his belt and puffing his chest out like a rooster. "Think to scare me with some foul creature of the wood, do you, cow?"

Werian leaned toward her, his gaze trained on Odo. The look was as deadly as a scar wolf's fangs. "Shall I end him, or would you like the honors?"

"Do not get into the habit of stealing my joy."

She grinned, feeling victorious, then looked to Odo. He deserved a spell that would either kill him or render him harmless to everyone else forced to cross his path. Maybe something to shut him up. Remembering the witch's style of spell casting, Rhianne tried her best.

"Strength to weakness, sour to sweet. Bind him, break him. Ancient witches, do as you see fit." The wind took her words and spun them through the air like autumn leaves.

Werian whispered in her ear, his warm breath prickling the skin of her neck. "That did not rhyme."

Pushing her hair away from her face and doing her best to hide the delicious shivers rioting down her body as a result of his nearness, she raised her chin. "I don't think it's entirely necessary."

He winked. "I hope not."

A cracking sound issued from the wand, and an ebony cloud filled with golden sparks unfurled. Like flaxen thread around a spindle, the magic twisted its way around Odo, whose mouth hung open in shock and fear.

Rhianne's stomach clenched at the sight of her work, of the ancient witches' work. Werian put a gentle hand on her back but kept his gaze on Odo.

The brewer's hulking arms flung wide, and his hair rose like he was in the middle of a great storm. He had broken her hand with no care as to whether she would ever be able to do more than beg again, and he'd left her to the scar wolf to die a vicious death alone in the wood. Odo had to be stopped.

Finally, he fell to the ground, legs folding like a traveling chair.

"Did she kill him?" a child asked behind them. It was the baker's eldest. "I hope so."

Rhianne grimaced, but she was fairly certain Odo wasn't dead. She held her breath until his chest moved and affirmed her guess. "We don't kill unless we must," she said to the children. "Remember that."

Odo sat up, blinking and scratching his neck. As he found her in the growing crowd—a group that kept their distance from Werian and her—his shifting eyes stilled. His lips pulled away from his teeth, and his face reddened, nearly going purple. He stood, wobbling a bit, and pointed.

His mouth opened to shout, but nothing came from his lips. He couldn't speak. Tearing across the ground, he raised a hand to strike her, but she didn't flinch. Somehow, she knew there was no need to fear him. Not anymore.

Werian bared his incredibly white teeth—Sacred Oak of the Wood, they were sharp—but he didn't come between her and Odo, and she was glad of it. This was her fight.

As Odo's arm worked to hit her, purple splotches rose in his red cheeks, and his muscles quaked. The villagers' silence cloaked the roadway, and Odo's straining sounded all the louder for it.

Werian's eyes sparked like a flint. "Try to strike me instead."

The fine hairs on Rhianne's arms stood straight up. Good thing he was on her side.

Shifting focus to Werian, Odo stuttered. "No." His hand went to his mouth. "I can talk."

Rhianne laughed, the sound cutting. "Only when you're acting like a human and not an ass."

Odo hurled himself at Rhianne again, but he hit an invisible wall and bounced backward. Shouting, he whirled, and his gaze caught on another victim. The innkeeper's slim daughter stood beside the one family member she had left after the war—her little brother. Splashing through a muck-filled puddle, Odo ran at her, his eyes bulging.

Rhianne aimed her wand, and a flurry of lightning thundered at him. The magic hit his back, then morphed into a black cloud that swallowed him whole. Strange and sparkling threads flared inside the dark plume of smoke as the tempest of power churned. With a final crack of thunder, the cloud spit Odo out, and he sagged into the mud, face-down.

"You did this to yourself." Rhianne's hand shook, her healing arm throbbing in time with her pulse.

The villagers didn't say a word of thanks, but the innkeeper's daughter lifted a hand, her doe eyes blinking back tears.

Rhianne gave her a nod as she and Werian mounted their horses and headed toward the road and its patterned shadows. The forest was alive with the chirrups of red-backed shrikes, and the tree branches bowed respectfully to Werian as the horses went from a trot to a canter. The rays that pierced the forest's canopy glinted off his rune amulet.

At a steep incline, the horses slowed, and Rhianne's curiosity got the best of her. She reached over and ran a finger along one of Werian's horns. The surface was smooth and cool. He growled and closed his eyes, pausing beneath a beech tree that bent its leaves toward him like a supplicant.

Her heart kicked her ribs. She had offended him, hurt him. Maybe both. "Should I not touch you like that?"

When his eyes opened, they were black and burning. He leaned close, his voice but a whisper. "Not unless you want to delay our visit to Khem with lovemaking. I might let the world burn for a day of pleasure with you, but I'm guessing you're more practical than me."

A dimple appeared in his cheek. The very ends of his eyelashes were a dark purple. She hadn't noticed that earlier. His thumb dusted over her forearm, barely touching her skin and electrifying a path to the crease above her elbow. Pulse galloping, Rhianne swallowed as every inch of her body heated like banked coals blown back to life.

She fought to breathe normally, then responded with a cracking voice. "Of course." She coughed a laugh. "We must hurry to Khem." Even if they didn't have the kingdom to save, her nerves would never allow her to *enjoy such pleasures* yet. She had to grow more comfortable with him first.

She gathered her courage and looked up to meet his liquid gaze. Goosebumps rose from her navel to her toes. His cheekbones—sharper than a human's—caught a spear of afternoon sun through the trees as he took her chin gently and lifted it. The foreign Naroniti spices he wore spun around Rhianne's head as he placed a kiss below her jawline. She shivered delightfully, and she nearly slid from her saddle.

Here was her fated lover. Her mate. Her match.

Joy danced through her blood as he lowered his head, locking his gaze on hers, a question in his burning eyes. "Are you second-guessing our match?"

How could he think that? Well, she had to put this fear of his to bed.

Leaning precariously from her horse's back, heart thrashing like a storm-tossed sapling, she pressed her mouth to his. Heady as rose water and poppy's milk, his lips opened to her before the tip of his tongue swept over hers. A deep noise reverberated inside his throat and chest, beast-like and thrilling. She nipped his lower lip and left him panting.

Breathing heavily, she pulled away and attempted a cocky grin, an echo of the one he'd worn at their first meeting in the castle's courtyard. "Are you finished worrying about my commitment now?"

"You are a terrible monster," he said, slow as honey.

She pinched his chin. "I'm *your* terrible monster." She nudged Storm with her heels and glanced at Werian.

Hands clasped over his heart, he sighed dramatically. "I am doomed."

She held up her wand. "And I'd thought this new magic would be my greatest weapon."

He caught up, eyes sparkling and tousled hair tangling around his horns. "Your lips are the most dangerous of poisons, entrancing me, sentencing me to a lifetime of servitude to your every whim."

Rhianne couldn't fight her wide grin. "Don't fret, my prince. I too shall serve you."

A laugh erupted from Werian's mouth, and his throat bobbed above his cloak's silver clasp.

She led the way down the road, easing Storm into a canter again. Her heart sang. Was this love? Not yet. But maybe someday. Maybe someday *soon*. Regardless, Werian and this new life had been well worth the risk.

A raven's call scattered chills across Rhianne's skin. She jerked the reins abruptly, and Storm stumbled to a stop. As her heart cantered faster than the horses' earlier pace, Rhianne ran a hand down Storm's neck. "Sorry, lovely. Sorry."

She twisted to look at Werian, who peered into the dead crown of a large white oak. He was whispering something, but she couldn't make out the words. They had a distinctly fae quality to them, blurring and dancing over her ears.

The raven shuffled its wings. "I see it now," she said. The bird was glossy black like Werian's horns. "Do you think that was our first warning? The first of our three calls?"

His large hands rested lightly on his pommel, his neck stretched long as he kept watch on the raven. "Well, I don't think he was asking us to dinner."

"No need for lip, Prince." When he glanced her way, she gave him a withering look. "Do you sense anything odd about the creature? Could the Matchweaver be here somewhere?"

Ice touched the back of Rhianne's neck, and she turned

Storm. The trees beyond the road swayed gently in the easy wind, but no other birds made a sound.

"It's a shade quieter than it should be," Werian said, easing Moon between Rhianne and the oak that held the raven. "Let's be off, aye?"

"Couldn't agree more." Rhianne urged Storm into a canter once more, praying to the Source that the cold at the back of her neck would fade.

CHAPTER 12
WERIAN

Werian finished the last of his watered wine as they trotted along the wagon-rutted road leading to the Sea's Claw. The moon glowed over a copse of beech trees. "What do you think of stopping there to fashion our disguises?"

They couldn't ride into the tiny village of Fieldbloom—where he often stopped for sleeping—as Werian and Rhianne. They had to become Shadowhood and Merewyn.

"I can braid my hair in an odd manner." Rhianne's quick fingers were already untying the ribbon that held half of her hair away from her face. Dark circles marked her eyes, evidence of her frightening day and the hard ride this far. He longed to take her into his arms and croon fae mate songs into her ear until she fell asleep against him.

"Good idea." Werian put a hand on each of the horses and healed what he could of the wear and tear of the road. Storm's flesh shivered under his touch and Moon nickered, encouraging Storm to remain peaceful and stand still.

"Are you helping them travel like this?" she asked. "They've been incredible so far."

"I am, but they do need rest. You do as well. I can heal, but nothing replaces sleep. We'll stop at my usual spot. It's not far. We'll sleep for a few hours, then ride out again." He reached for her hand. "May I?"

"Heal me?" The curiosity in her look made him want to crush her to him, to protect her from everything dark in the world. His mother's viciously beautiful face flashed through his mind. The Fae Queen would be a problem soon. There was no way she'd accept Rhianne as his mate. His mother didn't appear evil to those on the outside of the court's inner workings. She certainly did good things from time to time. Her darkness showed in cleverly managed situations in which she enabled others to cut her enemies with words or blade. Oftentimes, she even wanted to see suffering from persons who weren't her enemies. Was she horrid all the time? No. Was anyone? But she was most assuredly on the darker side of the spectrum than the average fae.

Once, his mother had organized the kidnapping of a Khem noble's daughter. The talk was that the girl was an extremely rare type of witch with no power of her own but who increased the magical strength of those around her. It had been frightening to see the poor girl shivering in the corridor outside his mother's room, her hands bound and tears silver on her cheeks. Werian had only been a boy then, but he remembered it like yesterday.

"Yes," he replied. "Please allow me to heal you."

A shy smile graced Rhianne's rosy lips, and he ached to kiss her. Instead, he closed his eyes and let the energy of

97

the earth and his own body buzz through him. He funneled the power along his fingers and across his palms, allowing the magic to flow to her. She made a small sound like a gasp, and when he opened his eyes, she was smiling, her rainbow-hued eyes shining with the moon's pale light.

"I liked that," she said, an edge of mischief in her voice. It stirred his desire, but they had to hurry.

He tipped his head to her, then began on his glamoured beard while she wove her hair into four braids, one above each temple and two higher up. She then worked them together at the crown of her head.

"Very nice," he said. "Shows off your proud cheekbones. My match has lovely bone structure."

"Yours isn't too bad either."

His lips parted in shock, then she winked, and he had to chuckle. She was already using his arrogance to tease him. *She might just survive this match yet.*

He removed his fine velvet vest and tucked it into his saddlebag, then turned his cloak so it showed the green side, tucking the hood at his neck properly. Once he had his eye patch in place, he held out his hands. "Ready for me to give you a new face?"

She lifted her chin to him and set her jaw. He took that as a yes and proceeded to change her multi-colored eyes to gold, her chestnut hair to obsidian. It had been kind of her to braid it and save him the energy of a more challenging glamour. He wasn't sure if she had done so on purpose. She probably knew little of the work it took to do fae magic, but nonetheless, it was a nice dose of energy she'd saved him.

"How do I—" She broke off her statement and pointed to the tree behind him, her eyes like wagon wheels.

He spun to see the beech painted by moonlight, the leaves ghostly pale and shuddering in the autumn breeze. "I don't see anything..." But then he did.

The base of the trunk and the roots above ground were black. The moonlight couldn't touch them, so dark was the color.

He crouched to touch the area. "What is this?"

Rhianne's hands pressed against her stomach, her simple dress bunched between her fingers as she stared at the trees surrounding them. "It's... it's spreading."

Werian stood and watched as the black color seeped from the ground and up every one of the beech trees. Long streaks of the ground had gone dark too, the moon's light banished like it couldn't exist in the same space.

Rhianne fisted her hands, her new golden eyes narrowed. "It's the old Matchweaver. She's draining the land." She snatched her wand from where she'd tucked it into her belt and held it aloft, expression fierce.

A chasm of fear opened inside Werian's chest, and a chill unlike anything he'd ever felt swept through him, shaking his bones.

Wand in hand, Rhianne eyed the darkness. "I'll try to help the earth fight it."

He said a silent prayer.

Whispering her words, she held the wand over the blackened roots. Charcoal-colored smoke billowed from the rowan wood and swirled atop the fouled spot of land. "Banish the evil, push back the dark. Overcome, defeat—"

The earth shook and sent Rhianne flying backward, and he caught her under the arms.

"Well, that didn't work," she said as she stood and dusted herself off. Her words were casual, but her pale cheeks said she was equally as frightened as him.

"Forget sleep." The raven's call echoed in his head. "We must go. Can you manage it?"

Rhianne nodded and began to mount. He gave her a lift, then once he was on Moon, they set off at a canter. If the horses could last, if he could keep them running with his fae power, then they could be on the ship and sailing by midmorning.

Was the deathly black spreading throughout Lore this very moment? Would people die if it reached them?

Cloak fluttering behind her, Rhianne led the way down the road. He kicked Moon to catch up with her.

"Do you know any folklore about a well in Khem?" he asked. "Or anything about witches and wells?"

She shook her head and pushed a lock of black hair that had fallen from her braids behind her round ear. "I know of the ancient Source's spring, a well that was in Illumahrah."

Werian nodded. "Of course. Supposedly, our spirit agate is a byproduct of the well's change in form after it sank beneath the forest floor in the time of goddess Vahly and the god Arcturus."

"Yes, when they had their children," Rhianne said. "I don't recall their daughter Lyra having anything to do with the well or spirit agate though. Or Khem for that matter."

"But she must have. Or her direct descendants," Werian said.

The goddess Lyra had been the first witch. Khem was known for producing an incredibly powerful witch every few generations. He'd nearly been forced to marry one when he was too young to even consider marriage. His mother had hired someone to kidnap the poor witch woman because the witch was like a piece of spirit agate herself, increasing the strength of any being's magic tenfold when they were in her presence. Thankfully, the innocent witch had escaped his evil mother's wicked plan.

"Werian, look." Rhianne's gaze drew his toward a hill slicked in that same darkness. "Do you see the shapes there? Can you tell what they are?"

He squinted, then his heart fell. "They're dead deer. A stag and two does." Rhianne glanced at him, worry pinching her eyes, and he blinked, fear wrapping his body in invisible ice. "What will be left of Lore by the time we return?" he said, his voice sounding strange to his own ears.

"We can't waste thought or worry on things we can't control, my prince. We must focus on our goal—the well in Khem. One thing at a time."

"So just ignore the quickly encroaching darkness that slays everything in its path. Of course. Easily done. It's only life or death." He cocked an eyebrow at her.

She laughed sadly, and they increased the horses' pace, the sea salting the wind and telling them they neared the coast.

CHAPTER 13

RHIANNE

Rhianne's mouth refused to close, so shocked she was at all the new sights and sounds of the Sea's Claw. Squawking gulls wheeled above multicolored, three-storied shops and thatch-roofed homes squatted along winding, cobblestone streets. There were so many people!

She and Werian had dismounted to lead their horses down the crowded roads and she had to keep reminding herself to hold the reins.

Every type of voice imaginable shouted and sang, called out for attention or shooed a street dog. Fallen apples rolled from a turned cart and a cluster of bright-eyed children lunged for the red prizes. A woman with braids like bread loaves above her ears ran them off with a broom, snapping at them about thieves and honor. Their shoes showed signs of a fine cobbler's work —no heels flapping around or split stitches that she could see.

Werian's glamoured face appeared in front of her. "Are you examining footwear, Merewyn of the Bones?"

"Oh, uh, maybe?"

Eyes dancing with mirth, he covered his mouth, then spun on his heel to keep on walking the sloping path toward the docks. The tops of masts cluttered the end of the road like an over-pruned forest.

Rhianne smacked his shoulder. "You'd be peeking at shoes too if you'd spent your entire life as a cobbler."

"I assure you I would not. While I respect the profession wholeheartedly, after all, I adore these boots for both comfort and style, I can't fathom a desire to study strangers' feet out of mere curiosity."

She glared. "Footwear, even at its basest form, is art. Take a closer look." She set her foot in front of his and tripped him. He bent forward, his face close to the street, then regained his balance too quickly to fall.

Laughing, he pinched her elbow gently. "You naughty thing, you. Though I suppose I deserved that."

When they arrived at the docks, he waved a hand grandly. "Welcome to the home of the *Nucklavee*."

Werian's ship was a dream.

The sides were as smooth as a river stone, the decks smelled not of fish but of lemons, and the masts stood straight and proud. The ship was named after a northern province folkloric demon, *Nucklavee*, and the gold-painted letters glittered in the sunlight. A woodworker had carved a siren into the ship's prow; the siren's long hair wrapped around her body, and her lips parted in song. The craftsman had sculpted a demon's skeletal face beside the siren, and its bony arms encircled the woman's waist.

Rhianne wasn't sure who was killing whom in the macabre scene, but it was fascinating nonetheless.

"When you're finished crawling all over the ship, darling, I'll introduce you," Werian stood as Captain Shadowhood beside his crew. They'd been wildly busy when she had first arrived, pulling ropes this way and that and loading crates on board. She hadn't noticed the men had stopped working and were staring at her as she studied their ship. "This is Merewyn of the Bones, a witch and a... let's call her a woman of business."

The crew smiled at that, eyes gleaming and gazes straying to the wand she had tucked into her belt.

"Oh, sorry. I didn't mean to ignore you all," she said. She hoped they would like her. She'd never had friends, and a longing to have them accept her nearly brought her to tears.

Climbing down from the ship's side, she slipped, and Werian was there faster than any human could've been. His eyes narrowed, then he laughed, covering the sudden silence of the crew.

"Don't fall in here, love." His voice was smooth and confident, his hand warm and strong. "This harbor holds the deepest water you'll see near a landform. Aside from the one strip of coral there, the sea drops down and down and down. It's how we can dock this size of ship so close to Lore."

The crew had to have seen the way Werian moved. He said the massive man named Little John was the only one who knew his secret, knew Werian was actually a fae prince, but that seemed unlikely. These men might pretend they believed their captain was human and non-magical, but Rhianne would've gambled every last hair on her head that they knew he was fae.

A diminutive fellow with hair like straw came forward. "Nice to make your acquaintance, Merewyn. I'm Eamon. Captain here says you have had dealings in the western provinces."

Sweat rising on her brow, Rhianne recalled the story they'd concocted. She wasn't used to lying even if it was for a good cause. "Aye. I'm a bit of thief myself," she whispered, giving them a wink. She glanced at Werian, whose mouth quirked up to one side. "I'm not much with a blade, but I'm a fair shot with the bow."

"I'm Beorn," a sturdy, dark-skinned man said. "Can you work magic against foes?"

Rhianne's skin itched. She wasn't sure she'd ever get used to having magic. It was a glorious power, but she felt like she was walking on a newly frozen pond. The surface would break beneath her at any moment, and she'd drown. She cleared her throat and aimed to sound as self-assured as Werian always did. "I can, but it does take a bit more energy from me than shooting an arrow."

The crew's murmurs said they had heard as much about witches and magic in general. "Water mages are like that too, eh?" Eamon asked.

"They are," Werian said. "Now allow me to introduce everyone, then we can be on our way. There's no time to waste."

After Rhianne and Werian explained the darkness that was spreading and how they must find a well in Khem, the crew set to preparing the sails and hauling up the anchor. They left out some details of the story.

"They don't need to know everything," Werian whispered as he joined Rhianne in looking into the compass box at the helm. "Just enough to have them working fast and true. No need to fill their heads with too much and overwhelm them."

"I think you should tell them all," she whispered back. "They seem quick-witted, and someone might have a better idea than us as to what to do when we reach Khem."

"What if the Matchweaver's spirit somehow finds them? What if they know too much, and she wishes to suck the information out of them?"

"I love that you want to protect them, but they're in this up to the neck. No use in keeping bits and pieces if they might see us more quickly to a favorable conclusion."

Werian made a shallow bow. "I humbly disagree. But I do promise that if we become stuck fast in our plotting, I'll talk to the crew in more depth and troll their minds for ideas."

"Good. Now, what kind of food do you have on this ship?"

"Does playing the role of thief make you hungry?"

"It would seem so."

Werian whirled and raised a hand to Little John. "Once we're out of port, how about some of your famous hotcakes?"

"As you wish, Captain!" Little John tugged at the lines, his eyes covered by a mop of dirty hair.

Soon they were sailing the open sea, and Rhianne realized that a person could fall in love not only with strangers, but with things that had no heart.

The sea fully enraptured her.

. . .

AS THEY SAILED TOWARD KHEM, RHIANNE PEPPERED Werian with questions.

"Why is it so much warmer in Khem than in Lore?"

"It's something to do with the air flowing across the ocean," Werian said. "John could explain it better than me."

Biting her lip, she pondered the layout of such an island. "What are their houses like?"

"Beautiful. Because of the temperature, they don't build walls. They use linen curtains instead, tied between pillars of white stone. The curtains billow like sails, and it's the most wonderful thing to lie on a pile of down pillows and drift to sleep after an exciting day."

Rhianne didn't care to ask what he had done on such pillows or with whom. A spark of jealousy burned her, but she snuffed out the flame, knowing he was with her now and that was all that mattered.

"What do they wear?" she asked. "Will we look out of place?"

"People sail from all over the world to trade in Khem, so we will only be yet another group of travelers. The Khem folk wear tunics that go all the way to their ankles, and they don boots that are open at the toe and heel. And they wear kohl around their eyes. It's a dark cosmetic much like what Balaur elves wear during their wedding ceremonies."

"Did you attend Princess Aurora and Prince Filip's wedding in Balaur?"

"I did. It was...fascinating," he said.

"In what way?"

He licked his lips and raised an eyebrow. "Their ceremony is far more visceral than the Lore ritual."

"I don't know what that means."

He grinned. "I love that you don't pretend to know what you do not. I wish more folk were like you, in that regard especially." He touched her back, almost absently, like he didn't realize what he was doing. But she certainly did. His fingers on her spine ignited a delicious heat that spread down her back and sped up her heart. "Visceral," he said, "well, I mean to say the Balaur wedding ceremony involved blood, plant poison, furs, fire...It engaged more deep, physical feeling than the Lore ceremony, which focused on explaining the gods and goddesses and the bond the two would create. Lore was more about the intellect. Balaur made one *feel*."

A question popped into her head, but she bit it back, afraid it was too early to ask about a fae wedding and what kind of ceremony that might be. Delight rushed through her at the thought of someday marrying Werian. But would he truly want to? After the truth of her basic humanness grew dull? How could he want a simple woman like her? Granted, she had magic now, but he was otherworldly in a way she could never be. She liked herself just fine and didn't feel unworthy of him, but she knew for certain she wasn't as exciting as he was. Surely, he'd grow bored of her and find himself tempted by past lovers.

Pushing that worry away, she asked a new question. "What language do they speak in Khem?"

"Ours," he said. "The language originated in Khem,

actually. Their accent sets their speech apart from yours and mine though."

"Your fae accent is different from mine too."

"Is it?"

She nodded. "A little. You trill your Rs a tiny bit, and your vowels sound...juicy."

A dimple appeared in his cheek. "Juicy?"

"Like you've just eaten a ripe strawberry and the shape of it sits in your mouth as you speak."

A laugh danced from his lovely lips, and she longed to kiss them. She inhaled his spicy scent.

"Is that where you get the Naroniti spices?" she asked. "In Khem?"

"Yes. I like burning their incense in my chambers when I'm at the fae court."

"I like it," she said, feeling bashful.

He pulled her to him gently and looked down at her. He was so tall. "I'm glad you do, my fated match. I'm very glad you do." His thumb brushed her chin, and the tip of his tongue touched his bottom lip as he gazed at her mouth like he was thinking of kissing her. Every inch of her skin tingled.

"Don't forget the gryphons." Eamon's bright face appeared at Werian's shoulder.

Werian rolled his eyes. "Don't forget that some conversations are private."

"Sorry, Captain." Eamon wound a thin rope around his shoulder and elbow.

"Wait. Gryphons?" The half-lion, half-eagle creatures were only in stories, right?

"Yes, gryphons," Werian said. "They have a small population of the rare creatures on the western cliffs."

Rhianne's mind spun. "I thought that was all just children's stories! How big are they? Do the Khem folk ride them like goddess Vahly once did?"

"No, they have no tie to humans, elves, or fae anymore. They're wild now."

Rhianne sighed, leaning on the side of the ship. So the gryphons were much like the dragons, except for Prince Filip's Jewel and the large Wylfen dragon the Lore army had defeated during the last attack. *Feral and most likely better off without us*, she thought.

"I hope we can see one," she said quietly.

"Keep your eyes alert." Werian gazed across the water. "We aren't that far from Khem, and I've seen two or three flying this far from their nests during the last few years."

A FEW HOURS LATER, LITTLE JOHN SAT ON A BARREL OF spirits and lifted a conical instrument to his lips.

Werian had pulled his dark hair into a low knot, and though Rhianne wished she could see his pointed ears and fae horns, he was still incredibly handsome with that trim beard, strong chin, and that roguish eye patch. He offered her his hand, his green cloak flapping lightly in the salty wind off the sea. "When Little John plays the shawm, it is ship rules that all will dance."

"Don't have to ask me twice."

Rhianne's heart soared as he twirled her into his arms. She'd often practiced steps to village reels in the secret of the workshop's back room. No one had ever asked her to dance. Werian took both of her hands and thrust her to one side of him, his hip touching her waist. With a stomp, he released one hand, then spun her around.

Eamon's feet moved quickly over the deck, boot heel to toe.

With one hand still linked with Werian's, she mimicked the movement. It wasn't too different from what she'd learned around bonfires in Tyreh. Werian's eyes sparkled with delight and he copied her footwork, his steps far more graceful than Eamon's or hers. He rolled her into his embrace again, and she leaned close.

"They'll know you're fae if you keep that up," she whispered.

He chuckled. "I'll blame their silly thoughts on the rum."

"What is rum?" she whispered back.

"They'll know you're no sea thief if you don't know about rum."

"Enlighten me."

He reached back toward Eamon, who handed him a wooden cup of whatever was in that barrel. "It's not wine, but it'll make that head spin just the same."

Werian handed the cup over, and Rhianne took a sip before returning it. The liquid burned its way across her tongue and down her throat, but she managed to hide the surprise well enough. Hopefully.

The lilting, trilling notes from the shawm curled through the air as Werian linked an arm in Rhianne's. He danced faster, his black boots moving back and forth in a simple pattern that she mimicked, though not shifting quite as quickly as him. She tried to keep up and finally matched his pace, and he laughed. He took her by the waist, lifted her, and turned her around so that her back pressed against his stomach. Every muscle in his torso seemed to tense between the slim layer of clothing between them, and her fingers longed to run along the lines of his body. Instead, she spun and threw her arms around his neck. If they kept dancing and perspiring like this, she wouldn't be able to stop herself from trying to kiss him. She didn't want him to find her so easy to catch. The fun was in the hunt, at least that's what her gut told her. She wanted to see Werian struggle for her attentions.

She raised her voice and lied, "I once had a crew who challenged one another to archery contests on board. Would the crew of the *Nucklavee* be interested?"

A wicked grin tugged at Werian's lips. "What do you think, men?" he asked the group at large even as he kept his hot gaze on her face.

"Aye!" the crew shouted.

Beorn opened a small door near the rear of the ship and heaved out a crate of wrapped bows and arrows.

Against everything her body asked, Rhianne pulled away from Werian and went to fetch a bow.

CHAPTER 14
WERIAN

Werian hadn't realized how crafty Rhianne would be. The little fox was teasing him, pulling away and challenging him to an archery contest on his own ship. He loved it.

Eamon finished painting green circles on a burlap sack. He scrambled up to the crow's nest, pounded a nail into the side, and hung the makeshift target. The rest of the crew found seats on crates and barrels or leaned on lines, bets spoken from the sides of their mouths. Werian, Little John, and Rhianne climbed the short steps to the quarterdeck, each outfitted with a bow and three arrows. Rhianne's rosy cheeks lifted as she smiled and tested her bow.

Beorn raised his hands. "Contestants will have three shots at the target. Best shot wins all."

"What do we win?" Little John asked.

"Glory," Werian said at the same moment that Rhianne said, "Respect."

She glanced at him, laughing, then stepped forward to take the first turn. With a strength he didn't realize she had, she pulled the string back, the point of her elbow straining against her tunic's sleeve and her face deadly serious. She loosed the arrow and hit the center green circle to a chorus of cheers.

Werian bumped her gently. "All right. Move aside and stop showing off."

"Oh?" She chuckled. "Because it's your turn to do so?"

"Indeed." He aimed and let his first arrow fly. It split hers cleanly down the shaft. The crew began to sing.

"Shadowhood, born of the forest,
He is the arrow,
The weapon's sharp tip.
If you cross him,
You'll find sorrow,
And your girl at his lip."

A stone settled in Werian's stomach. "Forgive their enthusiasm." He didn't like the wariness in Rhianne's eyes. Surely she wouldn't give him up because of his reputation with past women.

Her eyebrow twitched, and she turned away from him. "John, your turn."

John glanced his way, and Werian nodded. John took his shot and hit the mast below the crow's nest, the blue fletching of his arrow the same color as the afternoon sky.

The crew howled, and Werian set a hand on John's shoulder. "You don't need to try to make us look good. We can handle that on our own."

John punched him in the stomach. Werian huffed a breath and coughed a laugh, knowing he deserved it.

Rhianne eyed them like they were naughty children, which Werian supposed wasn't too off the mark, then she aimed and let her second arrow zip through the sails' lines. The yellow-fletched arrow hit the outer edge of the green circle.

Werian tsked. "Oh, no. Was that first shot beginner's luck, then?"

She walked past him and not-so-lightly stepped on the toe of his boot. "I'm just helping you feel better about yourself."

John covered his mouth, shoulders shaking.

Werian grinned and loosed his second arrow without bothering to stand still to do it. The arrow split Rhianne's once again. Her gasp turned him around.

He stood close and leveled a hot look on her. "I am your hunter. I go where you lead, little fox." The flush that crawled up her throat and spread over her cheeks sent a sharp thrill through him.

Her eyes were half-lidded. "Fox have teeth, Captain Shadowhood, so do be careful."

Gods in the skies, how he wanted her. How had she lived for so long in a tiny village with no adventure to speak of? She was a bright flame, ready to burn, to run wild, to set the world on fire. No wonder the people there had shunned her. They'd had no idea what to do with her heat, her ferocious joy of being alive. It took everything in him not to throw her over his shoulder right then and there and take her to his cabin. But he was no brute. He would wait for her, and if he won her, the delight of their union would be all the more pleasurable because of the waiting.

Little John hit shy of the center the next two turns

while Rhianne's arrow hit right outside the center. Werian landed his last next to hers, just to show her he was chasing her.

John shook his head. "So I get all the glory and respect, then?"

"And the rum!" Eamon lifted a small barrel above his head.

The archery contest turned into a drinking competition that Werian and Rhianne bowed out of, choosing instead to play a game of dice with the quieter members of the crew.

It was easy to forget that darkness was spreading over Lore even now and that death would reign if they failed in this quest for the next Matchweaver. But Werian pushed the thought away again and threw the dice.

WERIAN STOOD AT THE PROW WITH RHIANNE, THE STARS shimmering like dragon scales and the moon a scythe. The salty wind turned, and behind them, Little John shouted a command to correct their course. Rhianne's glamoured hair was too silky to remain braided, and long strands flew around her heart-shaped face. The magic tugged at his energy, making him feel as though it were past time for some rest. It was far easier to keep a glamour on one's own body or even one's own possessions. Other people's energy tended to fight fae magic.

Rhianne stared out over the silvery waves. "I could sail like this forever."

"I'm glad you don't feel ill."

"Not at all." She stretched her arms wide and leaned

forward, closing her eyes and smiling. "Are you actually a pirate, or do you simply trade in spirit agate?"

"One illegal activity not daring enough for your fated lover, hmm?"

She straightened and tugged her cloak around herself, blinking up at him prettily. "I'm only curious."

"I believe that is your leading trait," he said.

"What's yours? Changing subjects?"

He barked a laugh. Such a clever woman. The ferocity from her true eyes glittered through her glamoured ones. "If I find a Wylfen vessel of lesser fighting ability in these waters," he said. "I attack. We claim all but what they need to make it home."

"What type of goods do they usually have?"

"Furs. Coin." He rubbed the carving Eamon had made above the ship's bulkhead last season. It was their crew's symbol—a skull and arrows. "Also wine and information."

"Information?"

"Aye. I can usually get one of the crew to talk about their king's plans. Nothing exact, mind you, but a general idea of if or when the Wylfen plan to attack again."

She swallowed and touched the wand tucked into her belt. "Please tell me they aren't going to invade anytime soon."

"From the little we've gathered, the king has gone fully mad. It's impossible to know what he'll do next. The only thing consistent is his hatred of magic. He imprisons all witches and mages who aren't wise enough to keep their inborn power to themselves."

"But he used a dragon during the last attack, and one of his men could communicate with it like Prince Filip."

"True. I had forgotten about that. It happened before the battle, and Filip told me the tale much later. Perhaps the mad king of Wylfen thinks dragon riding is not a magical power. Who knows?"

Rhianne shrugged and stepped closer. She shivered. He put a hand on her back, eyeing her warily. "Would you like to go to my quarters now?"

Her chest rose and fell, and she started to say something, but then closed her mouth again. He would have to be careful with this innocent woman. Yes, he was a bit of a rake, but the lovers he'd had were rakes themselves. He didn't want to break this woman's heart.

"I see that caution in your eyes," she whispered, glancing at the crew as if she didn't want them to hear. "And I want you to let it go. I might be new to love, but I am strong. I've been through a great deal of suffering, and I'm still myself."

He was humbled by her admission, by the clear way she saw herself, by what she had endured at the hands of men like Odo and folk like the superstitious villagers in Tyreh. He put a hand over his heart. "I will do my best to recklessly ravish and adore you, sweetling, if that is your desire."

Her cheeks flushed. "It is."

He held out a hand, and she took it, her fingers slightly calloused and slim. They were so unlike a fae's fingers, fae that worked little and didn't normally develop calluses because of their innate healing ability. But Rhianne's fingers were perfect. Their humanness pleased him in some undefinable way. Maybe because her hands showed the life she'd lived.

The crew parted to let them pass. Eamon whispered something to Beorn.

"Shut your mouth, Eamon," Little John snapped. "Get to the sails. This wind is angry."

The ship listed slightly as Werian opened the cabin door and led Rhianne inside. His small bed had a new coverlet in emerald green, and the curtains over the three round windows boasted gold-embroidered bows and arrows as well as demon skulls.

"I hope the skulls don't ruin the mood." He removed his eye patch and let his glamour and hers fade away. The relief was wonderful.

Rhianne touched her chestnut hair and her cheeks. "I'm me again."

"You were always you."

"I quite like the skulls. Reminds us that life is fleeting. Much more so for me than you, I suppose."

"We are not immortal. No matter what some say. But we do have long, long lives. And you will as well, if you so choose. If you keep spirit agate about your person, it will lengthen your life span, barring any illness or injury."

She stood at the windows, pulling back the curtain a fraction to peer at the sea. "Truly?"

Werian nodded. The magic of being fae and knowing what he knew felt fresh and good when explaining it to her. She made everything feel new.

He came up behind her and touched her cloak's tie. "May I?"

She nodded, her body touching his. Her gaze went to the corner. "How does a stove work on a ship? How does it not burn the decking?"

"You see the stone there?" He pointed. "The slabs are set on sand. Both layers protect the decking. The chimney passes through to the weather deck."

"Fascinating."

With her cloak on the hook by the door, he turned to face her. She sat on the bed and unlaced her boots. She was still shivering.

"Allow me. Once you're under that coverlet, you'll be warm as a summer day." He finished removing her boots.

She stood and removed her belt, setting her wand on the window ledge. The sea heaved, and she fell against him with a gasp. Her wand clattered to the floor.

Fire sparked through his veins, and the thrill of having her in this private room brought many fantastic images into his head. He could take it no longer. He crushed his mouth to hers.

She was both strong and soft in his arms, her waist small and her fingers tight on his shoulders. Her lips tasted of honey and apples, and every sigh from her left him breathless. He didn't know what to do with this feeling. It was so much...more than anything he'd experienced. His body and heart and soul roared to life like she'd used her newfound magic to revive him, to bring him into an existence he hadn't realized was possible. Every sweep of her lips across his, each touch of her palm to his cheek—it was all a wonder.

"Rhianne," he said, sounding painfully breathy and unlike himself. "You're the rake here, I'm afraid. I feel I'm completely out of my depth."

Her eyes were stars. "You feel it too? That rush? What is this—magic?"

She kissed him again before he could answer, and he smiled against her mouth. "It's fate, I suppose," he said. "This is what it is to be matched by the Mageloom. But there's no way it feels this good to everyone."

"No?" She kissed his neck, then threw her head back for him to return the favor.

He touched his mouth to her throat, then kissed the pulse beating beneath her skin. His body was aflame. Something about her scent, her warmth, made her completely impossible to deny, not that he would even try.

"Captain!"

Rhianne pulled away.

"Not now, John!" Werian nearly growled and tugged Rhianne back to him.

"Werian, the weather," she said.

Only then did he notice the ship had gone utterly still. His stomach dropped. Through the small part in the curtains, the sky blinked with distant lightning.

Desire and magic warring inside him, he waved a hand, fingers splayed, near his face, then hers, replacing their glamours. "Stay here," he said as he grabbed his eye patch and started toward the cabin door.

"Like Nix's burning flames, I will!" She threw her cloak back on and grabbed her wand.

Werian started to argue, but she'd used the dragon goddess' name, and it was the first time Rhianne had sworn. She obviously wasn't going to remain safe down here.

"Captain! The sky!" John shouted.

Werian tore the door open and raged up the stairs to

see a spinning tower of clouds whirling like a three-sided blade toward the ship.

"John, the—" He started to order them to tie up the sails, but they'd already done so. "Lash yourselves to something, men! That beast will do its best to rip us from the deck and tear us limb from limb. We will endeavor to make ending us as difficult as possible."

CHAPTER 15

RHIANNE

Rhianne never guessed she would die at sea. Until recently, she had been a cobbler who hadn't left her village, land-locked and completely ignorant of anything to do with the ocean. "I was just falling for you," she said as Werian lashed her to the mast, the rain pelting them.

"And I for you." His wet shirt stuck to his chest.

"No, I was talking about the sea."

He shook his head. "I'll try not to die from your words before the storm has its chance."

A hysterical laugh crawled from her throat, and she spat salty water from her mouth. "I only meant I love the sea, and it's already turning on me."

"The ocean, she is a fickle lover." The rain dragged Werian's hair over his sharp features, and water dripped from his trim beard. His eyelashes stuck together, thickening them and making it look as though he wore cosmetics.

The ship lurched, and the ties holding Rhianne bit into her arms and stomach. Her wand remained tucked into her belt, its tip pressing against her ribs. Could she do anything with it to help?

Clouds roiled overhead, lightning flashing in their black depths. Howling in her ears, the wind smacked the tied sails and tugged at any loose bit of cloth it could find. The spinning column crept closer, closer, its sound like a thousand galloping horses.

And then it was upon them.

The wind and the waves thrust the ship this way and that. Werian's face contorted as he shouted, Little John, Eamon, and the rest of the crew calling back, though she didn't see how they could possibly make out the words over the storm's noise. Rhianne shut her eyes against the wind and the spraying water, then the world turned upside down.

In the blurry dark, a crack sounded, and the ocean swallowed her down its cold and soaking throat. Currents dragged her toward the sea floor or maybe back up to the surface—she had no idea which—and her lungs burned as she fought a rough tangle of rope that held her boots together. The mast that had been at her back was gone, and her arms were free, but she couldn't get a good hold on the knotted rope at her ankles. Her lungs were going to burst, and her eyes beat like hearts in her skull as she tried so hard to see more than a lightning-painted glimpse of shapes that made no sense.

She refused to die.

Giving up on the rope, she used her feet like a paddle, drawing them back and forth, driving toward what she hoped was the surface. Still, she saw nothing that could be defined. Only a strip of light there. A haze of glow on something flat. Slight movement in the dark that caught a flash of lightning. Yes, she was moving toward the surface. Good thing too because her head was floating, and her lungs were demons made of fire fighting her from the inside.

A cold, hard object bumped her arm. She grabbed for it, snagging one of Werian's horns. He drove upward, and they broke the surface. Rhianne gasped, desperate for air, her fingers now digging into Werian's shoulders. The water crashed over her head, and water clogged her gaping, half-frozen mouth. She coughed uncontrollably as he threw her onto what had once been the door to his cabin.

"My boots are tied. Can you help me?" A cough stole the rest of her words.

Werian's head disappeared beneath the surface, then she felt his hands on her ankles as he worked her free.

The storm swept past and left a whipping rain and churning water.

Werian rose to the surface and laced an arm around her. "Can you keep a hold on this door? I have to find John." The fear in his eyes had her nodding even though she certainly couldn't hang on for very long. The ocean remained angry and wild.

He gave her one last stern look, then dove into the black sea.

She gripped the rough edges of the door's carvings, fingernails hot with the effort. The ocean pushed at her and tried to yank her under the water, but she kicked and gasped and held on. Her wand. Panic thrusting through her mind, she felt for the wand. If she'd lost it, would that mean all was lost for Lore? That the old Matchweaver would take it all and turn every living thing into darkness?

Werian's voice broke through the chaos of the dying storm. "John!"

Rhianne twisted to grab at the back of her belt. "Goddess Vahly, goddess Lyra, please..."

Her trembling fingers found the wand, only its very end still trapped by her belt. Relief poured across her heart.

The moon threw blue spears through the clouds to show Werian swimming between various members of the crew floating as they grasped barrels, planks, and other debris. Nothing was left of the ship.

"Here!" a low voice boomed from the distance.

Werian swam in the voice's direction, and the moonlight poured over John stretched out on what might have been the last of the main mast.

Shivering and coughing, Rhianne smiled. They'd survived. But how long could they float in the middle of the sea with no way of getting to shore? How far were they from Khem?

Werian swam back to her and pressed his lips against her temple. He shivered too, although he felt warm. "I always wondered when my crew would learn the truth about me. I didn't expect it to be so dramatic."

He was right. They bobbed nearby, and those who were alert stared openly at his horns and his two good eyes.

"You didn't think something to do with you would be dramatic?" She lifted her eyebrows. "Come now."

He laughed wearily and kissed her temple again. "I do

hope we live through this. I see our future filled with a scandalous degree of fun."

But as the night wore on and the crew's questions about Werian were answered, the silence of the open ocean deflated all hope of rescue.

"Do ships ever come through here, or are you the only one?" she asked Werian.

"This is a trade route. Someone will pass by." But she could see what he wasn't saying in the glint of his eyes. He didn't know when another boat might sail near them. And they certainly wouldn't see them at night. How long could they last out here with the cold slowing the blood in their veins and sharks swimming nearby?

She raised her wand and thought only the words, *Help us.*

CHAPTER 16
WERIAN

Werian winced at the astounding light blasting from the end of Rhianne's wand. "Light is good. Bringing a ship into being would be better. Have any of those up your proverbial witch sleeve?"

"I'm not exactly tip-top shape at the moment," Rhianne said wryly. "I have no head for magic right now."

"I'm sorry. I was only trying to lighten the mood." He pressed a hand to her back and healed her some. She needed rest though, and he did as well.

A shape appeared in the distance.

"It's a ship. Very nicely done, darling." His voice was raw from shouting for Little John.

The water sloshed around them as Rhianne gripped his hand. Her fingers were icicles. "I hate to disappoint you, but I didn't magic that out of thin air." She faced the oncoming ship and waved her arm. "Hello!" Her moonlit eyes were wide and hopeful. "They can pick us up!"

He shrugged. "Or kill us."

"I thought you were an optimist."

"I strive to be so. Sometimes reality ruins everything."

He'd seen vile ships of rough men on these waters more times than he cared to count. Of course, he could play out a strategy number five—fake an injury, then attack, but that was fairly exhausting on a good day, and today had not ended in a way he'd ever define as good.

His beautiful ship was gone, blasted to pieces. All those memories... All that cargo... The fish would enjoy a fine hoard of spirit agate tonight. He shook his head. What a waste.

He pushed the sadness away for the time being and reworked his glamour and Rhianne's too. Rhianne glanced at him, blinking as the magic stole her true features. Thank the god Arcturus it was night and none could see what he was up to. It would be difficult enough getting the crew to keep quiet.

"Who is there?" A young woman's voice carried from the quickly approaching ship. The vessel was larger than he'd first guessed it was, gleaming black under the moon and stars.

"There are fifteen of us," Rhianne called back. "We lost our ship to the storm."

Yes, it was a fine ship with trimmed, dark sails. No name marked the side, and the prow didn't boast a figure or any such decoration. "Hmm."

"What's the *hmm* for?" Rhianne asked as they kicked their way toward the ship where a rope ladder had been flung over the side.

"The ship is unmarked. Plain. These people don't want to be noticed."

"We can't be picky," Rhianne said.

"Truth."

Eamon and Little John made their way up the rope ladder first, then Werian helped Rhianne, and so it went until all were aboard. The crew of strangers were dressed in a fashion similar to the ship—no markings of house or country. Too clean as well.

This strange crew deferred to a redheaded woman and a young man by her side. Werian gave them a bow, then the *Nucklavee* crew and Rhianne followed suit.

"Well met and we thank you, fellow adventurers of the sea," he said. "I am Captain Shadowhood. This is John, my first mate, and Merewyn, my business associate."

The wind was a cutting reminder of what they'd lived through as well as the wet status of their clothing. The strange woman's red hair blazed around her face.

"We welcome you aboard. I'm Brielle, and this is my cousin, Gabe."

The young man nodded a mop of hair and bowed clumsily. He must have been painfully nearsighted, because he squinted constantly.

"That accent of yours..." Eamon scratched his wet head. "Is that Donan?"

The redheaded Brielle chewed her lip for a second. "Ah...we originate from all over the world. You know how it is with a crew." She smiled.

Werian's heart seized. Her words didn't possess the lilting brogue of Donan. The woman had the accent of a Wylfen. A shiver ran down his spine. He nodded twice to John, giving him the old signal. John purposefully tripped and knocked three *Nucklavee* men over due to his blessedly remarkable size. In the planned confusion, Werian slipped Rhianne's wand from her belt and hid it beneath his wet shirt as best he was able, stuffing it low into his trousers and hoping it wouldn't prod at things best left unprodded. He stepped between Rhianne and Brielle.

"We are incredibly grateful for the rescue," he said smoothly as John made a fuss finding his feet and apologizing to the strangers. "Could we trouble you for some dry clothing perhaps? And are you going to shore? Headed to Khem? I assure you if you can take us safely to Khem, we can repay your costs."

Little John glanced his way, brow furrowed. Werian never began a negotiation with an offer. He waited to see what the other party would suggest first. That was the way of those who succeeded. But this ship was captained by a Wylfen woman. Wylfen hated magic, and witches especially; he'd heard the king there had hunters who sought those with magic and brought them back to be burned alive. Brielle's people would destroy a woman like Rhianne. There was no winning here aside from getting off this ship as quickly as possible.

"Of course," Brielle said, extending her arms wide. "We have plenty of extra blankets and can lend cloaks and trousers as needed. Can't we, men?"

The crew murmured but didn't speak up. Perhaps because they only spoke the language of Wylfenden, the language of Lore's greatest and most ruthless enemies.

"And," Brielle added, "we happen to be on our way to Khem, so all is well on that account!"

A cheer went up from the *Nucklavee* crew, but it rang hollow. Werian could hear the trepidation—as well as the fatigue from the storm and the grief over their ship—in their voices. The nameless ship's crew began tending to Werian's men, and at least for that, he was truly grateful.

Rhianne leaned closer. "Did you..."

"Yes. I have your...special item. I will explain soon."

She turned away, acting like it was nothing, but the tightness in her back gave her away. She'd grown used to having witch power at her fingertips, and who could blame her?

Taking Rhianne's hand, Werian herded Brielle's cousin away from the group. "Master Gabe?"

"Yes?" Gabe smiled kindly. His accent was far thicker than Brielle's.

How naive were these two that they didn't think anyone would notice? The Wylfen weren't welcome in Khem. But of course, none would ask from where they hailed. If Brielle led the trip and the rest kept their lips sealed shut, she could possibly do as she chose in the markets.

"What is your business in Khem?" Werian asked, aiming for a light tone.

Gabe's eyes cut to Brielle, and he stammered, "My cousin is fascinated with artifacts from days of old. We are to meet an antiques dealer."

"Ah. Very interesting. We trade in simple spices. Nothing so exotic as the ancient mysteries." Werian laughed, and Gabe did too, though the man's chuckle was strained. "How long have you been at sea?"

Gabe swallowed, but before he could speak, a hand snatched him backward and Brielle appeared, her smile overbright. "You must get some rest," she said, gesturing to a door. "As the captain, you will take my first mate's quarters. You and your lady friend, if you both wish?" Brielle regarded Rhianne.

Rhianne eyed the woman like one does a snake partially glimpsed in the grass.

Werian didn't blame her. Brielle might seem robustly kind, but she was definitely from Wylfen.

"Any pets aboard?" Rhianne asked.

Werian exhaled so suddenly that he had to cough. Was she checking for scar wolves? Oh, gods save him from this brazen woman of his. She had no subtlety at all. If Brielle realized they suspected her secret, the Wylfen woman might decide they weren't worth the trouble and go ahead and kill them off now. His crew didn't have the strength to put up much of a fight after what they'd been through.

Brielle tilted her head. "We have one orange mouser. A cat named Linus. He won't bother you while you sleep unless you have food in your pockets."

Werian gratefully accepted a stack of dry clothes from one of Brielle's men, then the crewman pushed open the door Brielle had indicated.

"It's the room on the right," Brielle said. Then she left them to find their way.

Werian needed to talk to Little John and figure out the plan. They had transport to Khem, but how would they get home? For now, though, he had to rest and protect Rhianne in case these Wylfen decided to try to burn his witch.

CHAPTER 17
RHIANNE

Rhianne shivered as they walked into the cabin Brielle had offered them. A candle flickered in a thick glass cylinder on the wall of the cabin. A stove with a set up similar to the one that had been on the *Nucklavee* radiated blessed heat. A narrow bed sat against the far wall, and Rhianne was so exhausted, she'd probably fall asleep in it without even getting out of her wet clothing.

Werian shut the door firmly, then gave Rhianne his back. "Change now. Your hands are about to freeze right off your lovely body. I'm glad it's only autumn and not winter yet. You might have lost a finger or two to this mess of a quest."

She shivered so hard she worried her jaw would crack. "Thank you. I'm quite glad I don't have a laced-up gown like Brielle. My poor fingers could never manage it."

She thumped around behind him, shucking her simple, wet dress and underthings into a pile to the side of the door. Then she dressed in a dark-ruby-colored tunic and plain, homespun trousers that were a bit too big for her. The trousers had a tie at the front, and she knotted it as best as she was able. She set her sea-soaked belt, stockings, and undershirt across a metal contraption—set there, no doubt, for this exact purpose—to dry by the stove, wishing the contraption had enough bars to host her dress and cloak.

"You can take your turn now, if you like," she said to Werian.

Doing her best to keep her gaze away from him, she sat on the side of the bed and reached toward the stove as he hung his baldric on a hook and worked his wet vest and shirt off. Heat bled into her fingertips. Werian tossed the wand onto the coverlet beside her, and though she'd been trying very hard to keep her eyes averted, she glimpsed his bare chest and trim waist. His skin was as smooth as river stone, muscles cutting deep across him.

She forced her mouth to close, then took a breath and asked, "Why did you take the wand, anyway? What's wrong?" In her curled fingers, the wand was as warm as the heat from the stove.

"Brielle is Wylfen."

Rhianne's blood stilled. "No."

"Her accent gives her away. Her cousin's accent is even more clearly Wylfen. And you know how they treat those who have magic."

Goddess Vahly of earth, help her. The Wylfen burned witches. The stories went on and on about the horrific deeds perpetrated by their king.

A spark of hope lit up inside her.

"Could it only be the king who hates magic?" she asked. After all, she'd thought a fae prince was too far above her status to ever consider her as a love match, but here they were. "Maybe common folk, non-warriors, don't care about such things. As a simple villager, I never worried much about those beyond my ken. Perhaps Brielle and her cousin Gabe are the same?"

"I'm not counting on it," he said, starting on his trousers. She looked away. "I'll rest by the door. You sleep in the bed and rest your human body."

Taking her wand, she stared intently at the fire. There was a fully naked fae prince beside her. Breathing was impossible.

"You've been through so much," she said. "You deserve a night's rest too."

"I'm fae. I'll be fine."

She turned. He was tying on his dry pair of trousers as a knock sounded at the door.

"Captain," a voice said from outside.

Werian opened the door to Eamon's blinking gaze. The straw-haired lad looked like a startled deer, but Rhianne only glanced at him. The swooping line of Werian's lower back disappearing into his trousers drew her attention like gold draws a dragon. Her mouth was suddenly very dry.

"Captain," Eamon started again, whispering. "They are Wylfen, aren't they?"

Werian pulled the man inside and shut the door. "They are. But they've agreed to take us to Khem, and so we must take them at their word until they act as enemies."

Rhianne started to stand, but her legs were weak from the ordeal of the storm, so she plopped right back down onto the bed again. Concern flickered over Werian's features. "Aren't they always enemies?" she asked.

"Not on international waters." Werian threw his borrowed shirt on. It was far too short for him. "If my guess is right, which, of course, it is, then we are in the area of the great ocean where a person's place of birth matters little. Might, wealth, and wits rule this stretch of water—really, the same applies in Khem too, although they do have some local law one must abide by." He tugged the shirt off again, tossing it to the ground with a huff before winking at Rhianne.

Certain she was blushing to match a stupid cherry, she looked away, wishing Eamon would move along. Not that she had the energy for any mischief with Werian. She was fully exhausted. But then again...

"Little John says I'm to sleep outside your door," Eamon said.

"No, you know the truth of me now, friend," Werian said quietly. "Humans need far more rest than fae. Take our wet clothing and hang it to dry in the ship's kitchen or wherever you see fit, then go sleep with the others. That's an order." He handed the wet things to Eamon.

Eamon studied the place where Werian's horns hid under a glamour. "Aye, Captain. As you say." He gave Rhianne a nod then hurried away, Werian shutting the door for—hopefully—the final time tonight.

Rhianne left the stove to snuggle beneath the coverlet but took the down pillow from the bed and tossed it to Werian. "At least take this."

"Thank you, little fox."

Rhianne thought she said something clever back to

him, but she wasn't sure because the next thing she knew, it was morning.

Werian's thumb trailed down the side of her face as he sang in some strange language, his eyes shut. Light poured through a square window to slide across the sweep of his lashes against his cheek and the smooth line of his nose.

"Good morn, fair maiden," he crooned. The sound curled her toes. He opened his night-dark eyes. "Awake, for it is time to experience the adventure that is the island of Khem."

The strident call of a raven sounded. Rhianne met Werian's gaze as her heart jumped.

"We're almost out of time," she whispered, climbing out of bed to dress properly and tuck her wand into her belt.

"Well, we don't know that. It could be a moon before the raven calls again."

"That's some forced optimism if I've ever heard it."

"I told you. I do try for a determinedly positive outlook despite life's vicious side."

"I wonder how far the darkness has spread while we were dancing about and having a fine time. Werian, I feel terrible. I have been shoving my fears to the side to enjoy my time with you. I'm a monster."

He was at her side in a moment, his hands cupping her face. "I am worried too. Aury is dear to me, and if she were hurt..." Shaking his head, he sighed and shuddered. Then he looked her in the eye—strength and quiet wisdom seem to flicker in the dark depths. "But we can't weep and gnash our teeth the entire time we're trying to save everyone, now can we? We are moving as quickly and as best we can. Yes?"

She covered his hands with her own and savored the feel of his palms against her cheeks. "We are. I simply feel inadequate to the job, and with all those lives at stake... It's just..." Heat built behind her eyes, but she willed her tears away. "We can and we will keep on. May the goddess Vahly bless our quest."

He kissed her forehead gently, the scent of him rolling over her like a dream. "Well said, love. Well said." Fear darkened the tone of his voice. She was beginning to truly know him, to notice the nuance of his mannerisms. Never had she grown so close to someone so quickly. Perhaps this was another facet to being a fated match.

RHIANNE BID FAREWELL TO BRIELLE, WONDERING STILL what her story was. How did a young woman of Wylfenden end up sailing so far from home to seek ancient artifacts? And was that even the truth?

"I think she's of royal blood," Werian whispered after they bid the redhead and her cousin farewell.

"Why?"

"Because of the money and the freedom. A lesser royal could manage this. I seriously doubt any basic noble of that land could."

Khem's market was twenty of Rhianne's villages packed into one. The crowd parted for the crew of the *Nucklavee*, all eyes wary and children pointing. Food hawkers in sleeveless, black-striped tunics that hung to their ankles held out steaming vegetable pies for sale. Across the crowded street, merchants with kohl-lined eyes raised sparkling necklaces to the sun to tempt passersby. A spice seller used a pewter scoop to shift strongly scented cinnamon into a customer's green glass bottle. Two horses pulled a cart overflowing with textiles—pure white linen, purple-dyed bolts of a finely woven wool, and skeins of yarn the color of the sea at dusk.

"I want it all." Werian plucked a grape and ate it before the man selling them noticed. He chucked a small leather bag of coins at the jewelry merchant on their other side, then selected an earring with one large pearl hanging from its golden post. He popped it through his earlobe and grinned. "I look fantastic, don't I? What do you want? Choose anything, Merewyn of the Bones."

"Weri—Captain Shadowhood, we are not here to shop."

"Yes, I know. But it won't hurt to loosen the merchants' tongues by putting some coin in their pockets."

Fine. It wasn't entirely a ridiculous idea. "I want that sapphire, merchant." She pointed to a large, silver necklace from which hung a sapphire that was quite obviously false.

Werian leaned close. "You know that's painted, yes?"

"I do."

He nodded and blew a strand of hair from her neck, giving her shivers.

She paid the merchant more than he deserved. "Is there a sacred well in Khem?"

The merchant's brow wrinkled. "Not that I know of. Not much for prayers, myself."

Werian set his hands on the merchant's table of wares, the glitter of necklaces and bracelets reflecting the sun onto his face and the peek of his collarbone between his cloak's tie and his shirt. Rhianne swallowed. What would that soft skin feel like beneath her fingers? She shook her head. There was no time for such nonsense right now.

"Who around here does in fact care to pray regularly?" Werian asked the merchant.

"Couldn't tell you, Captain."

Werian's eyebrow slid toward his hairline, and the merchant went white.

"I saw what you did to that apple-seller, Captain," the merchant said. "I would never cross you. I'm telling you, I don't know anything about those who would visit a sacred spot, nor do I have any knowledge of a well. I'm sorry. Please." He shoved the bag of coins back at Werian. "Take the jewelry for free. It's on me, Captain."

Werian didn't accept the bag. He spun and set a hip against the table, crossing his corded arms. "Merewyn of the Bones, did you know that our friend here once dallied with one of the great family's distant cousins? She went on to study—what was it, merchant?"

What was Werian up to? The great family was the ruling house of Khem, ancient, powerful, and secretive. Growing up, Rhianne had heard countless stories about them and had guessed they were basically deities when she was young. Now she knew their prestige came from sharp-minded trade deals on their rare spices and the fact that they most likely had magic unlike anyone else.

The man stammered, his fingers gripping the dark blue cloth on his table of wares, "I can't speak to her, Captain. They would have me killed."

"Ah! I remember. She went into the study of sacred

objects, didn't she? Ancient findings from around the world and how they relate to the gods and goddesses?"

"She...she did."

Rhianne couldn't help but grin at how Werian had handled this. "Sounds like exactly the sort of person we need. Surely, the woman is permitted to speak to whomever she chooses. She is a royal here in Khem, yes?"

The merchant's face had gone bright red. "Please keep your voices down." He glanced behind him toward the dark entryway to a store where a woman hummed from the depths. "My wife would be appalled at my past. I was not chaste."

Werian smiled and patted the merchant on the shoulder. "Who is, my friend? Who is?"

"I am," Rhianne said, then turned to face the merchant. "And I believe the love of your youth might speak to another woman, don't you think? Especially if said woman had a particular shared interest?"

"Of course!" Werian clapped his hands together. "Where is she hiding these days, merchant?"

"I—"

The humor fell away from Werian's face, and his lip twitched, showing his fae teeth, so much sharper than a human's.

The merchant's eyes widened. "Zahra lives and works in the great family's first city. She has a small place by the sea. It's marked with a sign of a flower."

"See?" Werian said. "That wasn't so difficult, was it?"

"Abasi?" The humming woman popped out of the shop, and her merchant husband startled like he'd been poked with a sword.

"Nothing, sweet honey of my morning! All is well. No trouble here."

Rhianne and Werian walked away as Abasi's wife set her hip against the doorframe and crossed her arms. Her eyes were nocked arrows.

"I think we ruined his day." Rhianne stepped around a donkey that had stopped pulling a cart, much to his owner's chagrin.

"This day, yes. But tomorrow, when they've mended the tear, our friend will have a fine day indeed."

Rhianne frowned, lost on his meaning. Werian's mouth was suddenly by her ear. "I have much to teach you, love, and I can't wait to thrill you to your very soul." The moment he finished speaking, he stepped more quickly, and she had to hurry to keep up, her knees weak from the tone that had laced his words.

She pinched his backside and sped past him, chin raised. "Don't think you won't learn something from me as well, Captain Shadowhood."

He laughed loud and long and was still chuckling when they finally untangled themselves from the busy market to meet Little John, Eamon, Beorn, and the rest of the crew at the crossroads.

"Did the jewelry merchant give you the info?" Eamon asked, eyes eager.

"He did."

"So you drew out the questioning...why?" Rhianne asked.

"If I had come at the man too aggressively too quickly, he would've flipped away from us with some excuse. There were too many folk in that market to do anything overtly illegal."

"Like pounding a man's face in to get information."

"Exactly. You must dangle the hook, in this case, a bag of coins and a gentle question, then set the hook with a quiet, but very real, threat."

"Works every time." Eamon beamed at Werian.

Rhianne rolled her eyes at his hero worship.

Werian gasped. "Do you not think me quick-witted, Merewyn? Have you worked with better men than me?"

Of course, she hadn't. She'd lived her entire life in one wee village with no adventure at all to speak of. But she was playing the part of a thief and a woman who regularly dealt with pirates, brigands, and rogues such as Captain Shadowhood, and so she said, "Don't ask for answers you don't want to hear."

Little John let out a hiss like he too felt the sting of her barbed comment. Then the crew erupted into laughs. Werian's grin and the flash of interest in his eye told her he wasn't angry but tempted by her challenging statement.

"I must strive to impress this lady, my friends," he said to the crew. "She has high standards, this one!"

The road was hot, the air smelled of jasmine, and Rhianne felt terrible because while Lore died hour by hour, she was having the best time of her life.

CHAPTER 18
WERIAN

Werian raised his face to the Khem sun and soaked in the absolutely wonderful heat. Khem was too warm for most Lore folk, but the sun here energized him. Someday, somehow, he would live here.

Rhianne's melodious voice danced through the air. "What are we going to do about the trip home?"

"We'll do as pirates do."

"Steal a ship?"

Little John stepped closer and put a finger to his lips, his gaze drawing a line to a group of Khem nobility. The nobles' long, dark purple tunics nearly brushed the dry roadway. Rhianne nodded. A few minutes passed as they walked up a steep hill dotted with black goats and shepherds leaning on hook-topped staffs. Along the roadside, a woman in light blue stood at a wagon loaded with trinkets for sale.

"But how?" Rhianne asked.

Werian suppressed a grin. She was so curious. The woman could hardly keep from asking a question every moment she was awake. He loved her for it. "You're the one with a wand. You tell me."

A light laugh escaped her beautiful mouth, and she put a hand to her forehead. "I have no idea how to magically steal a ship," she hissed.

"I'd bet you could persuade someone that sailing us to Lore was in their best interest."

"And hold that spell throughout the journey? I doubt it. I do have to sleep."

"Let's see what you can manage." He spied Eamon in the jumble of his crew members walking in front of them. "Eamon!"

Rhianne shook her head. "Oh, no. Out in the open here? What if more Wylfen are around? I don't think this is a good idea."

"Thus begins every grand success. What's victory without risk and a nice dollop of completely impossible?" He snagged Eamon's shoulder and pulled the man closer to Rhianne. "Hold still, Eamon."

"What?" Eamon looked from Werian to Rhianne as they sidestepped him off the road a little.

Rhianne slid her wand from her belt where it had been hiding under the drape of her too large dress. She glanced at the road and the crew, then pointed the wand at Eamon. "You want Werian to have your trousers."

Werian barked a laugh and clapped his hands.

Rhianne scowled as Eamon froze. "Well," she said to Werian out of the side of her mouth, "it has to be something he'd fight against when not ensorcelled." She repeated what she wanted of Eamon again, and this time, Eamon didn't just freeze, he swayed. A nearly invisible mist of magic twisted away from the wand's end to wrap around Eamon's head.

Grinning like this was the best thing that had ever happened to him, he unbuckled his belt..

"I think it's working," Werian said, unable to stop laughing.

The crew circled back to see what was happening, Little John finishing up a vegetable pie and Beorn examining a new pair of gauntlets he must have purchased at the market.

"That's a fine pair of underthings, pirate," Little John said.

Slinging his belt over his shoulder, Eamon held the trousers out to Werian and smiled so widely a ship could've sailed right inside his mouth.

Beorn gawked. "Have you lost your head, Eamon?"

Eyebrows knitted, Eamon whirled to face Beorn. "The captain must have my trousers!" Spittle flew from his lips as he shook the trousers in the air. "The color is just right for his handsome eyes!"

Werian tsked. "Finally succumbed to my charms." He accepted the trousers with a bow. "Don't worry, friend," he told Eamon. "I'll walk with you until we meet the road that leads to the first city, then perhaps Rhianne can help you find your wits again." Then he leaned close to Rhianne. She smelled divine, of sun and roses. In her ear, he whispered, "Well done, my lovely witch. Very well done."

Her smile held the very essence of allure and attraction. "I'll ignore him completely for a time and see how the spell holds," she said, her voice taking on that calm, practical tone she used when thinking things out.

"I'm sorry?" Eamon rubbed his temples. "What did you say, Captain? Please keep my trousers. I'm not sure why, but you simply must have them."

Werian clapped Eamon on the back, and they continued onward. After about an hour, the spell wore off.

Eamon rubbed his face vigorously, then eyed Werian. "Why do you have my trousers, Captain?"

Werian fluttered his lashes. "You don't think they match my fine eyes so perfectly? Have you tired of my charms so quickly?"

Little John, Beorn, and the rest of the crew chortled as Eamon snatched the trousers from Werian's outstretched hand.

"You've all gone sun-mad," Eamon muttered, fighting a confused laugh. "Now where's my pie, Little John?"

John pulled a package from his bag and handed it over as Rhianne tapped her finger against her leg. "I wonder if persuading a person to give up a ship is more difficult than magically encouraging one to relinquish clothing."

Eamon stopped mid-bite, squinting at Werian. "What did you do?"

"There's a bit of leek between your teeth there, friend. Just there." Werian pointed. But Eamon only frowned. "Settle down, sailor. You helped us with an important experiment. I'll get you three pies when we're back at the market in payment for your troubles."

A wide grin broke over Eamon's face and Beorn patted him on the back.

. . .

THE ARCHES AND SPIRES OF THE FIRST CITY ROSE FROM the scrub at the end of the road. Dozens of loaded carts, snorting mules, stomping black horses, raucous traders, and richly garbed Khem residents lined up to enter the towering city gates.

"We should go to Zahra's house on our own, all right? I think it's best to keep a low profile."

Rhianne nodded. "I'm following your lead on this. Beginner pirate, here." She grinned at him, but the worry etched into the little wrinkle between her eyes dulled the light moment. She was thinking about Lore and the darkness and how much time they may or may not have left. He just knew it, because he was thinking the same thing.

Birdsong trilled from the palms lining the road, and Werian forced himself not to look up. Rhianne's gaze hit him. "Was that the third call?" The blush in her cheeks drained away and perspiration gleamed on her forehead, sticking little locks of her hair to her face.

"No. Definitely not." He had no idea, but if it had been, all was lost.

"How do you know?" she asked.

"That was no raven. Right, John?"

"Huh?" Little John frowned. "Oh, the birds? I think that's a pigeon."

May Arcturus bless him. "Exactly," Werian said. "Pigeons. Decidedly not ravens."

Looking like she might be sick, Rhianne took a labored breath. "It was the last call, Werian. You're trying to be positive again. We have to leave."

He went to the side of the road, out of the line of those

entering the first city, and waved at her to join him. "But what about finding the well?"

"If that was the last raven's call," Rhianne said, "then we have to hurry back to Lore and I must do what little I can with the powers they gave me. If we keep on searching here... This could take days, weeks even! Who knows? No, we are leaving." She spun and began to walk away.

He touched her arm and she stopped, her eyes large and full of panic and determination. She looked like a mother bear ready to defend her cubs.

"You tried your magic on the darkness," Werian said. "It had no effect."

Her hands fisted at her sides and she looked down at the dust on the toes of her boots. "But what if we're too late? We can't just leave them all there to die."

"We aren't. We're staying the course. This is their only hope. The well. You. The new Matchweaver rising at your behest or whatever madness the ancients had in mind."

She regarded the crew who stood in line, murmuring and shifting their weight. Then her shoulders twitched and she raised her gaze to meet his. "All right. We'll stay the course, Captain Shadowhood if that's your master pirate advice here."

"Does that feel right to you?" he asked quietly. "Don't just take my advice. Measure it inside. See if it feels like the correct move. Your gut can tell you."

With a breath, she nodded. "It does. We stay the course."

"All right then." He ran a hand down her back, wishing he could be in her arms, longing to take comfort from her courage. Fear was a whip cracking over his head, its tip lashing at his state-of-mind. "Men," he said, following Rhianne back to the crew, "you enjoy a fine afternoon in the city. We will meet up at the docks as soon as we complete our...errand."

"Aye, aye, Captain," they chorused.

"You sure you don't want another fighter at your back, 'Hood?" Little John asked.

"No, but I thank you. This will take delicate words and nuanced motivation."

John grinned. "Then I'm out for certain."

Werian clapped him on the shoulder, then led Rhianne down a winding road that branched away from the city. They walked in tense silence, worry for Lore and everyone in it a specter haunting their steps.

At last, a dusty, cobbled road led them along the sea cliffs to a two-story, whitewashed house.

"I see the flower!" Rhianne pointed at the garden wall.

Palm trees swayed overhead, their shadows taking the heat from the day. Out of those shadows, two large men appeared.

"Stop. What is your business here?" the older of the men asked. He'd shaved his white hair close to the skull and was rather intimidating for an elderly fellow.

"Why, we're here to visit Zahra. My sister here is passionate about ancient artifacts and wondered if she could speak to her simply for the pleasure of it."

Rhianne glared at him, no doubt an effect of the word "sister."

The guard nodded, the fire in his eyes dimming. "That would be in tune with my lady's wishes. I will ask her if she is of a mind to visit presently." He opened a bright blue door and left them with the second guard, who kept his distance. He was a young man, and he seemed rather nervous about the sword Werian had hanging from his belt.

Werian leaned close and whispered, "You must be my sister in case I need to use my male wiles to encourage Zahra to talk."

Rhianne cocked her head and gave him a dubious look. "Male wiles?"

He crossed his arms and leaned on the garden wall. "Yes. My maneuvers."

A tiny snort came from her. "Oh, I do hope she is interested. I'd love to see that in action."

"Teasing me now, are you?" He raised an eyebrow. "I could bring you to your knees."

Her lovely, smooth throat moved in a swallow. "I don't doubt it, but you can't right now. And so I shall continue the teasing."

Werian gave her a stern look. "There will be recompense for this treatment."

"I should hope so." Rhianne winked at him, and he broke, laughing.

She was such a fine match for him. How had he lived so long without her? It was amazing to see a person so ignorant of the world think so quickly and act so confident. She was an incredibly fast learner.

The old guard reappeared, then led them inside where they were met with the points of five swords.

CHAPTER 19
RHIANNE

Rhianne had her wand out before she could decide if it was a good plan or not. She kept it against her side, hiding it as best she could.

A woman in a long, white tunic appeared from the darkness of a corridor, then walked slowly past the stone pillars that supported the high ceiling. Her skin was the lovely brown of acorns. The sea breeze wafted through the mostly open room, tangling the ends of the woman's straight hair. She looked at Rhianne and Werian with absolutely no emotion in her eyes. "Who told you about this place?"

Werian spread his hands and grinned handsomely. "Lady Zahra, please. We are here to—"

"Tell me quickly, and you choose the way you die. Tell me slowly, and I choose."

Werian's charm wasn't cutting it, so Rhianne stepped in. "We have no desire to let anyone else know where you live. A female captain told us about you at sea. She picked us up when a storm destroyed our ship."

Werian glanced at her but kept his mouth shut. Rhianne figured Brielle could defend herself more easily from this bloodthirsty woman than a simple jewelry merchant.

Zahra tapped her nails on a golden belt that hung low on her slim hips. "Her name?"

"She refused to tell us. We were strangers at sea. It was very tense."

Narrowing her eyes, the Khem lady stalked toward them, gently pushing the guards' swords away as she passed through the group. "Tell me the color of her hair."

Rhianne had mentioned Brielle only because it was truth and therefore gave validity to their story, but did Zahra actually know Brielle? What were the chances? Steeling herself as Werian let her lead the way, she feigned confidence and said, "Red as fire, my lady."

Zahra's smile was sharp. "Come this way." She started toward a room where four low chairs with pale cushions made a circle.

Rhianne sat in the closest chair, but Werian remained standing. He'd gone very quiet, which was honestly rather frightening. He exuded danger, all of his playful bravado gone.

Zahra lounged on the largest chair, a gleam in her eyes Rhianne was fairly certain she didn't like. A curtain of tiny glass beads shifted behind Zahra, and Brielle walked in.

"Hello, again," Brielle said.

Rhianne began to sweat. "Hello."

"Now this is getting interesting," Werian said quietly.

Brielle took the seat beside Zahra. "You used my name to cover for another source who told you to find Zahra here. Tell us who told you."

Werian perched on the arm of Rhianne's chair. "I don't know his name. Some merchant at the market near the great port."

"Just what are you two after?" Zahra leaned forward, studying them.

Rhianne wanted to come clean, to tell the whole truth. But Brielle was Wylfen. How much power did Brielle have here? Werian looked at Rhianne and shrugged as if telling her the choice was hers. If she exposed herself as a witch, would Brielle strike out at her? In Wylfenden, they burned witches. Zahra was obviously close with Brielle. Would she support an attack against Rhianne? They certainly had enough men here to cut her down or to give it a good try anyway. But Brielle was here, in Khem, a land where magic was accepted and people from all over came to trade. That meant she wasn't your average, close-minded, murdering Wylfen, right? Well, no other clever plan had popped into Rhianne's mind...

Taking a deep breath, she decided to spill it all. "Lore is dying. The Matchweaver Witch's power has been given to me." She pulled out her wand, and both women across from her stared at it like it was a snake. "If I don't find the witch who is meant to be the next Matchweaver, our country, and possibly the land beyond our borders as well, will be swallowed by a magical darkness."

Brielle's gaze locked onto Rhianne. "I can see the fear in your face."

Werian stood, his hand on the hilt of his sword.

Brielle glanced at him, then looked again at Rhianne. "But you don't need to fear me. I suppose you've figured out my country of origin."

"You're Wylfen," Werian said quietly.

"I am. And I'm not supposed to be here. I tell you this because you have told me your truth. Now we all have secrets we're holding for one another."

What exactly did she mean? Yes, she was Wylfen, but she was here in Khem and Zahra didn't care about magic. What damage could one Wylfen woman do here if she had no swordsmen at her back?

"Why aren't you supposed to be in Khem?" Werian asked Brielle.

"Because I'm the king's third daughter and he would skin me alive if he found out."

She was a princess of Wylfen. Werian had been right when he'd guessed she was royal. "Then why come here?" Rhianne asked.

"Because I hate my country and my father. It's full of rage and close-minded fools. I long for knowledge, to see the ancient artifacts of the world before we broke into these kingdoms. The artifacts of the goddess Vahly, goddess Nix, the ancient Jade dragons too, it's fascinating and I think we can learn from the past. I hate what my father does to those with magic." Brielle's eyes shone and her body tensed. "It's not right," she bit out. "Any moment I can be away from him and from Wylfen is a treasure."

Zahra gave Brielle a sympathetic smile. "Brielle came here right after she docked. We meet once a year to go through the artifacts my team finds in the wilds of Khem, and she shares stories of the pieces she gathers around the world, particularly in the mountains that border Wylfenden and Balaur. Now, tell us more about this darkness you saw in Lore."

Rhianne and Werian explained the situation, though they didn't give their real names. Rhianne wasn't sure it mattered at this point, but Werian seemed inclined to keep that secret close, and so she followed his lead.

"There is a well," Zahra said. "It's beyond the Green Chasm."

"What's that?"

Brielle tied her hair up so it all sat directly on top of her head, then sat back and began toying with an emerald-encrusted dagger. "It's a divide in the earth where palms and thick vines thrive. Locals say the chasm is fed by no less than five springs. One of which feeds an ancient well. I've never been there."

"I have once," Zahra said. "With my aunt."

"Your aunt..." Werian started. Rhianne wondered why he cared.

"My Aunt Lapis."

Werian nodded, and Brielle began talking about the suspension bridge that spanned the chasm. He was obviously sidetracked by something to do with this aunt of Zahra's.

"Can we go now?" Rhianne said. "I'm up for crossing the bridge. We have no idea how quickly the darkness will spread in Lore. I need to find out who the next Matchweaver is and how to locate her before we have nothing to return to."

They were all in agreement. Once Werian had sent one

of Zahra's men to give a message to the *Nucklavee* crew, the party set out on four bay mares.

THE GREEN CHASM SHOWED ITSELF AS A LONG RIBBON OF bright color in the otherwise sandy, pale landscape. Palms grew along the edges, their wide leaves reaching down toward the rift as if they wished to join the crowd of jade-hued plant life. Wooden poles marked what Rhianne guessed was a suspension bridge, the type of crossing her home village of Tyreh had built across the river. Though the Green Chasm bridge wasn't close enough yet for her to see clearly, it had to be a thousand times larger than the one back in Tyreh. How did they construct such a thing? She couldn't imagine how difficult that would've been.

On the quiet, seemingly deserted road, Werian urged Rhianne's horse to slow using his fae way of speaking to animals. Ahead of them, Brielle and Zahra were busy talking about which one of the Khem nobles was the handsomest, and they didn't take notice of Werian and Rhianne's lagging pace.

"Unless you feel it's unwise," Werian said as he ran a hand over his horse's neck, "I'm going to tell them my true name."

"At this point, we're trusting them with everything else. But I'm curious as to why."

"I have history with Zahra's aunt. She was Princess Lapis of Khem once upon a time. It's a long story, but the important fact is I helped her escape a fate she didn't want."

"When?"

"I was young. Not yet mature. But I'm betting Zahra has heard the tale, and once I prove I am the one who aided her aunt, she'll be more inclined to help us find a ship to sail home."

"I thought I was to spell someone and do this in a witch-pirate manner. I was actually looking forward to it."

Smiling, Werian gathered his reins, his gaze on the sea beyond the cliffs. "We have our entire lives for pirating, little fox. Let me make this deal in a way that won't pull on your energy. You may need every last bit of it when we return home."

"All right, then." Rhianne bumped her heels against the horse's sides. "Lady Zahra, we have a confession to make."

Werian told them his real name and hers as well. Then he removed their glamour.

As Brielle gasped at the appearance of his horns, Zahra pulled her horse to a stop, then whirled the animal around so that she faced him.

"You were the fae youth who helped her escape?"

"I was."

"I remember her talking about those horns of yours." She put a hand over her chest. "I'm indebted to you by blood. My aunt was my heart mother."

"What's a heart mother?" It was a lovely term, but Rhianne had never heard it before now.

Zahra's eyes shone with unshed tears as her gaze moved from Werian to Rhianne. "She is the one I bonded with as a baby. My mother was cold. She didn't care for me, play with me. Aunt Lapis did. She visited me in secret when she was forced into hiding. It's quite a tale, but we must save that for another day. What can I do to repay this debt, Prince Werian of the Agate Court?"

"Loan me a ship for a year," he said. "I will return it sound and whole."

"Done." Zahra turned her horse and urged her mount into a canter.

"That was well done," Rhianne whispered to Werian.

Brielle's horse came alongside Rhianne's. "I am Princess Isabriella of Wylfenden. Royal to royal," she said to Werian. "I will hold your secret as closely as I do my own. We adventurers must stick together!" With a wink to Rhianne, she smiled widely, then nudged her horse into a full gallop, catching up with Zahra quickly.

"I'm beginning to feel ridiculously out of place in this adventure, if you want the truth from this cobbler's niece." Rhianne shook her head. It was unbelievable. The most shocking thing of all was how vibrant, kind, and lovely Brielle—Isabriella—was. A Wylfen princess befriending a witch and a fae prince... Who could have ever guessed it?

Werian snagged Rhianne's hand and brushed his lips across her knuckles. "You are the most graceful and noble of us all. Why else would the ancient witches choose you? You are the best of us."

A sigh left her, and she didn't even try to hide it.

But then, someone screamed.

CHAPTER 20
WERIAN

Werian's heart flipped. He kicked his mare and had her at a gallop before he knew what was happening. At the edge of the chasm, Brielle's horse stomped, and Brielle herself was on hands and knees holding out a branch for Zahra to grab. The bridge was hanging by just one of its ropes and Zahra was hanging onto the side of the chasm, only her one hand and part of her head visible from Werian's position.

"The bridge wasn't sound," Brielle said, looking up at him, her eyes wide. "Zahra tried to stop her horse, but it threw her. Help me!"

The spooked horse trotted beyond a cluster of low scrub, ears laid back.

Eyeing the frayed end of one rope tied to the metal loops on the support posts, Werian leapt from his mount's back. He gripped the last bit of whole rope holding one side of the suspension bridge. Below, Zahra had managed to wrap an arm around one of the bridge's wooden slats knotted into one hanging section of the bridge. The deep green of the chasm seemed an impossible distance away. Zahra's eyes were wild, sweat glistening on her brow.

"Hold on. I'll pull you up." He began winding the rope, one painfully difficult loop at a time.

Brielle blinked at him, her branch idea forgotten. "Fae strength," she whispered.

Rhianne's horse drew close, sending up a cloud of dust as Rhianne quickly dismounted. Wand up, she looked to Werian with fierce eyes. "What spell do you suggest?"

"You're the witch," he coughed out, struggling to slowly but surely bring Zahra up.

Zahra shrieked, and Werian was tugged forward.

"Stop!" Rhianne shouted, and magic wrapped him like strong arms, holding him back from the deadly drop.

He pulled back on the rope, dropped to sit, and wedged his feet against a half-buried boulder.

Brielle looked over the edge, her red hair flying in the updraft from the chasm. "She's lost hold on the slat and only has the rope. Rhianne, please!"

Rhianne was trembling.

"You have this, fox," he said. "Be clever. Don't let anything get in your way."

Wand aloft, Rhianne stepped right up to the edge and pointed her wand down. "Rise, rise, let not the blood of first royals die. Power in this earth at my feet, help me save your lady of Khem."

A tremor vibrated through the ground, and Rhianne jolted like she'd been struck by lightning. Lavender clouds of magic spun away from the wand, and then Zahra was floating at eye-level with Werian, her limbs swathed in sparkling purple.

Brielle and Werian reached for Zahra and pulled her to safety. They collapsed in a heap, Rhianne smiling down on them.

Zahra stood, dusting herself off. She bled from a cut on her arm and one on her head. "Thank you, witch. Thank you very, very much."

Brielle wrapped Rhianne in a hug that seemed equally capable of comfort and strangulation.

"Easy," Werian said, touching Brielle's shoulder.

Brielle pulled away, her smile wide. "You're amazing! I've never seen anything like that!"

As Brielle went to tend Zahra's wounds, Werian set a kiss on Rhianne's temple. "You are a wonder."

"It's the power of this place, I think. I felt so much strength from the very ground itself."

Zahra patted Brielle's hand but eased her away. "I'm fine." She turned to Rhianne. "It's the nearness to the well, no doubt. Old power sits here. In the land. In the water. The Source hovers close to those with the magic in their bodies and souls."

Werian felt energized. "This is wonderful. I have great hope you'll find all the answers at this well, Rhianne."

She looked out over the chasm. "But how do we reach it?"

He gathered the horses' reins. Zahra's mount had tangled itself in some dead vines near a cluster of bushes so he had Rhianne hold the other horses while he freed the trapped animal.

Nodding in gratitude, Zahra took her mare's reins from

Werian. "It will take ten days or so to walk around to a crossing point."

"We don't have that kind of time," Werian said.

Rhianne moved her wand from hand to hand, pacing. "I could raise the bridge?"

"That should be a statement, not a question, love. You can do quite nearly anything, I'd guess." He handed off Brielle's horse to the redhead.

Walking once more to the chasm's edge, Rhianne pointed her wand. "Come to me," she whispered, the sound oddly echoing, louder than it should've been. Chills spread over Werian's skin. He was glad she was a person of ridiculously upstanding character. If someone less worthy, maybe someone as roguish as himself even, had that kind of magic, all sorts of madness would be unleashed on the world. And that was exactly what was happening in Lore, of course. The Matchweaver had this level of power, and she was draining the life from the land, and maybe its people too. He shuddered, a renewed sense of urgency flooding his veins. "Is it working?"

Like charmed Khem snakes, the tattered rope ends that had held the suspension bridge across the chasm rose from the divide to hover before Rhianne.

She lifted her chin, eyes sparkling. Werian had to admit he was just a tiny bit afraid of this side of the fox.

"Come to me. Mend for me. Find your purpose and fulfill it, or you shall burn," she whispered, her voice echoing oddly again.

Smoke rose from the wand's tip, deep black and acrid in the salt air. The ropes shivered, then reattached themselves to the metal loops. The supporting ropes found what slats remained and wound themselves through small holes before knotting tightly of their own accord.

Extending her wand arm, Rhianne shouted at the chasm, "Strengthen and hold, be our support, or suffer my wrath!"

A bright purple and gold light flashed along the full length of the bridge.

Rhianne tucked her wand into her belt and dusted her hands like she'd been working the stables instead of doing the impossible. "That should do it."

Zahra and Brielle laughed, their eyes wide. "I can't believe what I just saw," Zahra said, shaking her head.

"Even after you were lifted into the air?" Brielle asked, her hands on her cheeks.

"I was distracted by nearly dying," Zahra said. "I was fully aware for that bridge trick."

Werian gave Rhianne a bow. "Can your bridge hold the horses, or should we tie them here?"

"I think we should go on foot. I'm new at this, remember."

Zahra and Brielle murmured their amazement as they lashed their horses to a towering palm's trunk. Werian and Rhianne tied their mounts to a cypress, then started across the bridge. Zahra and Brielle followed.

"I can't say I'm not nervous," Werian said.

Rhianne glanced over her shoulder, her nose wrinkling. "About the bridge? Me too."

"Yes, about the crossing, but I was talking about you."

"Me?" Rhianne's fingers moved along the bridge's ropes, her feet quick on the slats, lightly stepping over the places where no wood remained.

"I don't think you realize this, but you're probably the most powerful witch in the world right now."

"I won't be once we find the real witch, the one the ancients wish to take the Matchweaver's place."

"Still. You are delightfully scary, my love."

She laughed at that, and he grinned at the warm sound of her joy. She was such a dichotomy of innocence and danger. It was a concoction he found particularly attractive, and he meant to show her exactly how fond he was the very moment they were alone.

CHAPTER 21
RHIANNE

R hianne followed Zahra's steps through a winding, stone-lined path. Palms cast shadows over the royal lady's dusty tunic and shaded the rocky alcove at the end of the path.

"I have heard many tales about this well," Zahra said. The gold bracelets at her wrists jingled lightly.

Werian and Brielle were talking quietly several steps behind Rhianne.

"Would you tell me one?" Rhianne asked.

"It is said," Zahra started, "that this well was once under the ocean. Before the time of great change during the reign of the goddesses and gods, when Vahly, Arcturus, and Nix roamed and worked their elemental magics. The water goddess Lilia found it, it is said. And when it retreated into the earth, Lilia passed to the next life."

"How did it end up here?" Rhianne asked.

"I don't know. The stories say the earth exploded in flames, shifted, and reformed. I suppose the well reappeared during such an upheaval." Zahra knelt and picked something up from the sandy ground. She handed it to Rhianne.

"A shell."

"A very, very old one. It's not simply been dropped here by a sea bird. The essence of the shell has been replaced by minerals from the earth."

Rhianne marveled over the way the earth had saved every ridge and slope of the shell. "Lovely." She sat it on a patch of wide-leafed grass near the path, then caught up to Zahra.

"We're nearly there. Can you feel it, witch?" Zahra's tone was quietly respectful, her dark eyes curious.

Rhianne could indeed sense a difference in the air here. It was heavy, perfumed with a scent not too different from the Naroniti spices Werian liked. The leaves on the low trees boasted a brighter green than seemed possible. The color nearly hurt her eyes. Orange and pink blooms burst from their branches.

"I do sense the sacred aspect of this place," she whispered, feeling the urge to keep her voice down. She ran a hand over a palm tree's trunk, the bark rough and smooth in turns.

Zahra stepped aside to let Rhianne pass. The alcove at the end of the path had been hewn from natural rock and was protected by walls of hand-shaped stone, perfect circles of the same white rock as the pillars in Zahra's home. Under the alcove's arched entrance, a pool of dark water sat utterly still.

A strange sensation spread over Rhianne's body, the fine hairs on her arms standing on end.

She could sense Werian's presence behind her, though he remained silent. His scent was on the air, and she inhaled it for comfort.

Large shadows suddenly cloaked the ground. "Step back," a deep voice said from above.

Three gryphons with male riders landed between Rhianne and the well.

Werian shot forward, his bow drawn and an arrow nocked before she'd even raised her wand. "Who are you?" he demanded, his glare as sharp as his arrow's tip.

A man with a sleeveless tunic that showed a myriad of tattoos—similar to the one female fae warriors had—dismounted, but Rhianne could only glance at him. The gryphons were amazing. Their heads were those of blue-gray eagles, their bodies of tawny lions, and paws as large as a king's platter threw clouds of dust into the air. The one nearest snapped its yellow beak, and Rhianne stepped backward, Brielle catching her arm and hissing something in another language—perhaps Wylfen.

The tattooed man walked up to Werian until his chest was but an inch from the nocked arrow's tip. "You must leave. This is the well of the goddess Lilia, and you are not of her blood."

"All blood is mixed with those of the old water folk." Werian lifted the bow so that the arrow skimmed the man's neck. "What nonsense are you going on about?"

"Lilia's power runs through those of the master water mages. Only a master water mage may visit this site. Or a soul that passes the test of the sea."

Rhianne pressed Werian's arrow so that he lowered the weapon. "I was called here by the ancient witches who created the Mageloom. We mean no harm to this sacred place."

"Even so, we will not let you touch the well until you have passed the sea's test."

The man turned, nodded to his fellows, then in a flurry of movement, the man's gryphon had Werian pinned to the ground with one massive paw. The second gryphon plucked Rhianne's wand from her hand with its massive beak, and the third creature stood on hind legs, cornering Brielle and Zahra against the stone wall.

"I am of the great family," Zahra said calmly, sounding both reluctant to bring up her rank and far less frightened than Rhianne felt under the threat of these giant creatures from the old stories. "I respect your commitment, but you are in the land of my family's reign. I order you to release us."

Werian's gaze flicked from Rhianne to Zahra like he had some sort of plan to move the moment her threat worked. Rhianne really hoped he did, because she had no idea what to do to escape this. Even if they broke free, she had to access the well to fulfill her quest.

But the three men didn't react to Zahra's order. Instead, they tied Rhianne, Werian, Brielle, and Zahra at ankle and wrist, then threw them in front of the gryphon's saddles like grain sacks.

Rhianne's stomach clenched as the gryphon ran and leapt into the air. The well faded from sight as they flew higher. They landed gracefully on a spit of sand where the waves were gentled by a corridor of high rocks just offshore. A longboat with carvings of gryphon wings along its sides sat on the sand, just out of the heavier waves' reach. The men unloaded Rhianne and the others, untied their ankles, and, keeping their prisoners at sword point, forced them into the flat-bottomed longboat.

"Why don't you simply overtake them with your fae strength?" Rhianne whispered as they were shoved to a sitting position in the empty boat.

"I don't want to ruin your chance to discover what you must at the well." Werian's cool gaze cut across the men's backs as they secured a rope through Zahra's and Brielle's bindings, lashing them together then did the same to Werian and Rhianne.

Rhianne fought the fear growing inside her chest by making a mental list of possible outcomes. "Being cast into the sea with my hands tied isn't helping my chances."

"No, but at least we're not dead." Werian lifted both eyebrows.

Fear wrestled down her logic. "Can we perhaps raise your goal here? I'm aiming for alive *and* escaping. Even if we manage to get back to shore after this ridiculous test of theirs, who knows if they'll allow me to do anything?"

The gryphons loomed over the boat, gazes sharp and beaks sharper.

"No one knows." Werian shrugged. "But they do seem honorable."

Rhianne's mouth fell open. Honorable? Because tying them up and keeping them from saving Lore was respectable? "Did you hit your head when the gryphon took you down?"

One gryphon leaned forward and set his paw on the boat's side. The craft lurched, then the only one of their captors who had spoken clicked his tongue, and the beast backed away obediently.

"Just as I won't argue with Prince Filip, who has a dragon on his side, I'm not starting a fight with a man who can direct a gryphon that specifically."

"We don't have time for this."

"What is the plan here, masters of the well?" Werian asked loudly.

The leader, or at least Rhianne guessed he was the leader, turned, still showing no emotion on his face. "If the ocean brings you back to Khem alive after you experience the encounter, then you pass goddess Lilia's test."

"The tides do as they always do," Rhianne said, suddenly more annoyed than frightened. It was a nice change, and so she held on to the feeling. "This is foolish."

Zahra squeezed her eyes shut momentarily. "Encounter? What will we encounter?"

Shaking, Rhianne tried to take deep breaths and remain calm, but this test was ridiculous. With no sail and bound as they were, how were they supposed to go out to sea, then return to shore? The sea waxed and waned, and it had nothing to do with what any of them deserved.

When none of them answered Zahra, she asked a new question. "What is the name of your group, if I may ask?" Her words didn't tremble at all. Rhianne wished her own voice would consistently sound like that.

"We are Defenders of Lilia, men sworn by an oath to protect the well, to die for its sanctity if the need arises."

The gryphons rose into the air to hover above the ground, their wings blowing down on them. One gryphon clutched the end of the boat with its talons. Rhianne's stomach turned as the boat shifted from its spot, grated across the sand, and was dragged into the choppy ocean.

"We'll be fine," Werian said.

"How do you know?" Brielle snapped, her red hair flying around her face. "What exactly do you see happening here other than us being set out to sea with neither sail nor oar?"

Zahra watched the two gryphons who remained close by the one directing the boat. The shapes of the Defenders on shore grew smaller by the minute. "Werian probably thinks he can charm the seas, hmm, Prince of the Agate Court?"

"See if I don't." He grinned, showing a sharp incisor.

The sea took over the gryphon's duty, and the creature released the boat, then flew back with the two others who were returning to their masters on the coast.

Rhianne closed her eyes, frustration bubbling under her skin. "I have no wand. Lore is dying as we speak. I hate to be a doomslinger, but this isn't going well, and I think you'd all agree."

"Doomslinger?" Werian asked. "I like it. Is that a Tyreh word?"

"Not the point here, my prince," Rhianne said through gritted teeth.

"They're the ones at fault." Zahra grimaced at the shoreline. "What kind of nonsense is this? They must realize we aren't common thieves trying to gather well water to sell off in the market. A lesser royal of Khem, a Wylfen-blooded princess, the Prince of the Agate Court, and a woman working with a powerful wand, not that they know what you can do, Rhianne.

But we are quite the crew, and I can't fathom their thinking."

Werian snapped the bindings at his wrists easily. "Zealots don't usually consider facts that others do. At the very least, they certainly know I'm fae and that such simple knots and rope can't hold me. And they recognize the look of you, Zahra. You are the spitting image of the great family's first queen. So their focus is on this test of theirs. They don't care who we are or what our purpose may be. They only want to see whether we fail or succeed."

Zahra shrugged. "What now?"

Werian tore the rope holding Rhianne's wrists, the action biting into her skin. She hissed in pain, and he quickly pressed his palm against the spot where the rope had rubbed her red. Healing warmth spread through her wrist, and she whispered, "Thank you."

His eyes glowed, and he gave her what felt like a secret smile. It was amazing she could still be so distracted and enamored with him out here on the wild ocean with no idea what challenge might be set upon them by the well's Defenders.

Werian kissed her forehead quickly, his lips hot on her skin, before he freed Brielle and Zahra.

The wind rose, salty and stinging, as Werian leapt into the water.

Rhianne gasped. "What are you doing?"

"I'll push the boat back to shore."

"But they're still there on the coast." Rhianne pulled at her braid, the tightness of the style suddenly incredibly irritating. "Their gryphons will simply shove us back out."

"Perhaps this is the way we'll pass their test. Besides,

I'm not sitting out here waiting. We have lives to save. Namely our own, then possibly everyone else's if we still have the energy."

"I heartily agree with that." Brielle glared toward the shore.

A low whistle carried on the wind and raised goosebumps on Rhianne's arms.

Brielle put a hand up to shade her eyes as she looked at the coast. "They're blowing a conch." She frowned at Zahra. "What is this about? I'm growing incredibly tired of these zealots."

"You and me both," Zahra said.

"If they wanted us dead," Rhianne said, joining in on the annoyance, "why didn't they just have their gryphons do the job when we were on shore?" Her teeth ground together as she looked down at Werian. Water lapped over the muscles of his arms and shoulders. A wave crested and splashed onto his horns and the side of his face.

Behind him, a huge, brown-and-black-striped fin speared the water.

Werian watched Rhianne's eyes go wide. He spun and a blur in the water headed straight for him. There was a flash of fins then sharp teeth sank into his leg, and bright red pain shot up his body.

"Werian!" Rhianne leaned over the boat's side, reaching out a hand.

He dropped beneath the surface. His blood trailed through the water, surrounding an unbelievable sight. Amidst the canopy of a lush, seaweed forest, a striped dragon with four limbs ending in webbed digits swam in slow circles. Three times the length of the boat, with teeth as long as daggers in its gaping mouth, the dragon shifted its fin-like wings and blinked at him.

You're beautiful and horrible all at once, he said, trying to speak to the creature's mind with fae magic. As far as he knew only Filip and one Wylfen soldier he'd heard tales about could speak telepathically with dragons, but why not try? Werian's blood unspooled around him, but his fae body worked on healing quickly. *I don't think I'd make much of a meal. I'm sure there are plumper fish for the taking, aye?*

The sea dragon swam forward, faster than thought, and gnashed its teeth at Werian's injured leg. Werian spun, narrowly avoiding the bite. Kicking hard, he drove upward, broke the surface, then veered toward the boat. He landed on board in a crouch and winked at a pale Rhianne.

She dropped to tend to his bleeding leg. "Your boot is ripped and your trouser leg too, but your body seems to be healing. What is that thing?"

He patted her hand, fear making his tongue taste metal. "I'm fine."

The boat lurched. Brielle grabbed the side and Zahra fell against the board that had served as a seat.

"Sadly," he said, "I don't think the boat will be fine for very long unless we find out how to scare off a sea dragon."

"A what?" Brielle and Rhianne said in unison.

"Look." He pointed at the array of black-and-brown scales riding along the water. The beast hit the boat with its whipping tail, and Werian grabbed a handful of Rhianne's skirts before she could tumble over the side.

Zahra put a hand on her neck like the very existence of the beast was choking her. "It's Apep."

"What is an Apep?"

"The dragon of chaos. The Defenders must have called it. The dragon longs only to destroy. It never dies. I didn't think the tales were true..."

Rhianne winced and shook her head. "They're always true."

The dragon's serpent-like, triangular head disappeared

under the surface, then the water foamed white. The beast banged into the hull, a cracking sound alarming Werian far more than the bite the creature had given him. He was an amazing swimmer, but he couldn't get all three women back to shore.

"Can anyone else here swim?"

Brielle shook her head. "Not that far in these waves."

Zahra nodded, but her cheeks had lost their flush. "I can. But please tell me we have a different plan."

Werian ripped his amulet from his neck. The golden oak, a symbol of the Agate Court, glimmered under the sun. He flipped the necklace to show the runes on the back, hoping the Sowulo and Eihwaz would increase his throwing ability through the air element. "Perhaps sea dragons are like their land cousins?" Holding the chain and leaning over the side, he dragged the amulet across the surface in an attempt to catch the dragon's eye. In his mind, he whispered to the dragon.

Come, lovely beastie. It's gold. Solid. Fae-touched.

Could the dragon hear him? Land dragons didn't hear fae mind whispers as other animals, so it was doubtful.

Apep's head burst through the water, droplets flying from its scaled lips and white teeth. Werian stood quickly, then threw the amulet as far as his fae strength allowed. The amulet disappeared in the distance.

The dragon leapt, then dove.

"Is it working?" Rhianne pushed her chestnut hair away from her face and stared.

"Perhaps?" *By the light of Arcturus, let it work.*

The prow launched upward, and all four of them fell, Werian wrapping himself around Rhianne to keep her from cracking her head. Water sprayed, drenching them as Apep rose from the water.

The dragon opened its jaw over the boat and let out a rattling hiss, its forked tongue shaking.

Chills ran down Werian's body as he looked around desperately for a weapon, but there was nothing.

With a sudden calm, Werian ignored the slathering beast whose head hovered over the craft. Werian took Rhianne's face in his hands. Her skin was damp and soft and smelled like honey. He kissed her sweet lips, savoring the moment. She kissed him back, but then pulled away. Her mouth opened like she was about to say something when a voice threaded through the sound of the water, gulls, and dragon.

Werian's arms dropped to his sides, his jaw slack. The singing was so painfully lovely. He had to hear more. His body felt warm and relaxed as he walked toward the side of the boat, searching for the source of the voice. He'd forgotten all about Apep, the serpent-dragon of chaos. He only wanted to wrap that song around him like a cloak and savor the pleasure of the sound forever.

CHAPTER 23
RHIANNE

Rhianne's body warmed to the singing. She followed Werian to the side of the boat, her mind in a delightful haze. She touched her arm, ran her fingers along her skin. She almost felt as though she were melting, and it was the most wonderful sensation.

There was a large splash in the water not far from where Zahra and Brielle stared in the direction of the singing. Ah, Apep had dived into the sea again and was also interested in the singer. Rhianne didn't blame the sea dragon. The lilting sounds seemed to prick at her heart, drawing her forward, promising every pleasure one could possibly imagine. One could think of nothing else but the singing.

"I see him." Zahra's black hair fluttered behind her as she pointed to a shape in the water.

Rhianne squinted, not at all concerned Zahra was climbing out of the boat. The man in the water had dark hair, broad shoulders, and blue eyes that shot bolts of desire right through Rhianne. Apep swam beside the singer, the dragon's tail slicing the waves gently. The beast made a cooing sound. The man held out a hand, and Apep swam away in the direction indicated, still cooing as it slithered through the ocean.

Zahra was swimming to the man, her slim, strong arms cutting through the sea to get to him. Rhianne wanted more than anything to join her.

Werian grabbed her arm. He had a hand over one ear, and his eyes were watering. His lips pulled back to show his teeth as he gritted out, "Plug your ears."

Why would he want her to do that? She turned to stare at the singer and smiled, feeling absolutely glorious.

Werian's hands covered her ears, and the singing grew muffled. She tried to pull at his wrists, but he was strong as an oak. Then her thoughts cleared. "What...what is happening?"

"A siren is out there. He saved our skin, sending Apep away, but now Zahra is swimming to him, and I don't know if he means her good or ill will. You must keep your ears covered."

She did so as he looked past her to Brielle, who was frowning at them.

"A siren!" Werian shouted as he ripped small strips of cloth from his shirt and stuck it in his ears.

Rhianne's stomach turned. A siren. A creature of folklore, one who could sing a song so tempting that a person could find themselves falling into the water, happy to drown as the siren's victim. Did sirens eat humans? What was their purpose in taking victims?

Rhianne went to Brielle, braced herself, then stuck a

finger in Brielle's ear, hoping to help her find a shred of clear-headedness. Brielle tried to shove her back, but Rhianne held her ground...

But the singing...

Her arms dropped. Forgetting Brielle, she went to the boat's side and lifted a leg, ready to jump in, to join the singer. Maybe she could beat Zahra and make it to the singer first.

Werian shoved something in her ears, and the world grew clear again. He'd stuffed rolled cloth into her ears and was doing the same to Brielle.

Brielle stood beside Rhianne as Werian leapt into the water.

"I cannot believe we've seen gryphons, Apep, and a siren all in one day," Brielle said.

"Me either," Rhianne replied. "I nearly went after that siren just like Zahra. That song..."

Brielle's throat moved in a swallow, and her fingers dug into the rope coiled on a post at the boat's side. "He won't hurt her, right? He drove Apep away and saved us. He won't take her under the water."

She sounded as though she were trying to convince herself.

"I'm sure you're right," Rhianne said loudly, her voice strange through the muffling effect of the cloth. She wasn't sure, of course, but making Brielle worry more about her friend wouldn't fix anything.

Werian used his fae speed to overtake Zahra and drag her back to the boat, kicking and swearing.

The siren gave them one last haunting look before he

disappeared under the water. Zahra immediately calmed, and they all helped her climb aboard.

Rhianne removed the cloth from her ears and shivered hard as Brielle thew her arms around the soaked and ashamed Zahra.

"It's not your fault." Brielle stuck the pieces of cloth she'd used to block her ears into the bag at her belt.

Zahra gazed longingly in the direction the siren had been. "I'm a fool." Her voice was a knife pointed at herself.

"No." Rhianne touched her arm. "It's an old magic tied to your lands. Of course you were swayed. We all were. Even Werian."

"Aye. I certainly was." He slicked the water from his hair, then squeezed the ends of the shirt that clung to his body, showing every line and curve.

That siren's song plus a drenched and gorgeous Werian made it extremely difficult to focus on the dangers of the moment. Rhianne shook herself.

"Are you all right, little fox?" As the other women spoke in whispers, he took her chin and lifted her face, looking at her intensely with his handsome fae eyes. Then his gaze grew sly, eyes half-lidded and lips sliding into a grin. "Ah, I see. The fellow in the sea roused your passion, did he? Well, I will have to assert my dominance in the realm of Rhianne's longings." His finger traced a line down her throat, between her breasts, then along her stomach. With a movement almost too fast to see, he set his mouth against her neck and ran the tip of his tongue over her collarbone. Her breath came in quick gasps.

"Werian. Not here. Not now." But part of her wanted to say the opposite, as mad as it was.

"Of course." He grinned wickedly, and her body trilled like a songbird. "Later, then, my love."

One of the gryphons flew from the shore, heading their way. Rhianne clutched Werian's hand.

"I'll glamour the image of a spear into my hand if it strikes. You take that moment of its distraction and dive into the water, but keep a hand on the boat."

"But the dragon and—"

"I don't think he will return."

She started to ask another question, but the gryphon arrived, blue-gray wings flapping above them. It dropped a white-and-gold-striped cloth into the boat, and Zahra picked it up.

"It's the Khem symbol of victory," she said.

Werian glanced at the cloth. "So the gryphon serves as our escort back to shore."

They sat on the boards across the bottom of the boat as the gryphon hooked its talons over the prow, and soon they were once again face-to-face with the Defenders of Lilia.

The Defenders silently nodded in unison, then the gryphons bent low for them to mount, blue-gray feathers dark against the golden sand.

"Now what?" If Brielle's glare were fire, the Defenders would have been roasted to their bones. "Are you taking us to the well or trying to feed us to another legendary monster? The decent thing would be to at least inform us of our doom."

"To the well, young wild one," the oldest of the Defenders said, gesturing to his gryphon as if he wanted Rhianne and the rest of them to mount up.

"I'll show you a wild one." Brielle stopped her tirade as Zahra patted her back. The redhead heaved a breath and rolled her eyes. "Fine. For you, I'll keep quiet. Only for you, Zah," Brielle hissed.

Both women set a foot on the wing of the gryphon belonging to the oldest Defender, then settled in front of the man, ready to take off. Werian gave Rhianne a hand up to the second gryphon, then he leapt onto the third and the party took to the skies. As they flew, Zahra looked toward the white-capped sea, wistfulness in her black eyes. That singer had truly affected her. Hopefully, she had the strength to keep from searching for him.

At the well, they dismounted as a salty wind tossed the palms overhead and curled dust into the air. The scent of fresh water touched Rhianne's nose, and goosebumps scattered across her arms, the sense of sacred magic heavy on her shoulders and head.

Werian linked his fingers in Rhianne's, and she savored the simple gesture of care. The tightness in his movements said he was growing more and more worried—most likely about when the next raven's call might sound or if indeed they had already heard it and they'd return to their home kingdom to see nothing but darkness and ruin. It was all she could think about.

The Defenders stood beside their gryphons and regarded Rhianne and her party. Werian gave a shallow bow, and Rhianne curtseyed even though she truly didn't want to. These Defenders had to approve of her so she could approach the well and move forward with the plan. Flying into their faces in rage wouldn't help the situation. She had a bit of fun imagining it though.

Beside her, Zahra nodded her head, but Brielle looked like a storm about to break.

Rhianne gave her a pointed stare, hoping she would cool down, but Brielle only whispered something that sounded like a curse in Wylfen.

"The sea brings you here, and so we permit your passage. You have passed the test," the Defenders said in unison. The leader went to his gryphon and rummaged around in one of the bags on the side of his gryphon's saddle.

Brielle muttered a few words, and Zahra whispered at her, perhaps trying to calm her friend.

Werian leaned toward Rhianne, his breath on her ear. "I wonder what they'll give you, darling." His voice held the spark of mirth. "A painting of their faces so you never forget their endearing smiles? Maybe a lock of each man's hair so you can sleep with it under your pillow."

Rhianne bit her lip to keep from laughing. "Hush, Werian."

The leader approached and opened his hand to show a small, silver necklace. "Because of the waters' blessing, we now give to you the amulet of Apep."

Brielle jerked her arm away from Zahra, leapt forward, and grabbed the leader's shirt. "How in the world do you equate a blessing with surviving a beast you knew was out there?"

The leader's face was impassive, but his eyes flashed with anger.

Rhianne and Werian moved to pull Brielle back, but the leader's gryphon snatched the back of Brielle's tunic and held her above his master's head.

Brielle swore again. "A flipping siren saved us, you idiot. And I'm sure he only did it so he could have a chance at our heads on his dinner plate! Let me go!"

"The siren king works in tune with goddess Lilia's seas as well," the leader said. He looked at his gryphon. "Take her to the bottom of the path to wait on the rest."

The gryphon trotted around the group, then took flight with a snarling Brielle still trapped in its beak.

It was almost funny. "You aren't going to hurt her, right?" Rhianne stared at the leader, hoping she was high enough in their eyes now that they would listen.

"The angry one will be safe while you approach the spirits of the well."

Zahra chuckled. "The angry one indeed."

Spirits of the well? What did he mean? Rhianne nodded and pretended she knew what he was talking about.

Werian's brow furrowed, and he glanced toward the sea. "Can you tell us anything else about the siren king? I had thought all true sea folk had changed a thousand years ago."

"We have seen five, but there may be more. Perhaps they only strive to stay away from humans in this age," the leader said.

Zahra swallowed and determinedly looked everywhere but the blue horizon of the ocean.

Sliding the amulet over Rhianne's head, the leader whispered a weighty phrase, like a spell. "This amulet gives you entrance to any great house in Khem, assistance at any Khem family's home, and the everlasting support of the Defenders of Lilia if you call on us."

"Thank you," Rhianne said. "Now, may I have my wand back?"

Once their weapons were returned to them and the Defenders disappeared into the sky, Brielle came marching up the path, still flushed and spitting mad.

Zahra snorted, then waved a hand, encouraging Rhianne to approach the well.

Everything went quiet. No bird song. Not a wisp of breeze.

Kneeling, Rhianne looked into the water, wishing for a moment she was a water mage like Princess Aurora and she could scry to see what her next move should be. But she was no mage; she was a witch, at least for the time being. She had no witch blood, so she'd hand off this power as soon as she found its true owner, the true heir to the title of Matchweaver. Hopefully, that witch would know how to break the dark hold the old Matchweaver had on Lore. The memory of that determined darkness spreading across the forest leeched into her mind. How had it deflected light? What was it exactly?

Only her face reflected in the water as she waited.

The well water rippled as if a breeze blew, but the air was unmoving. Normally, well water was dim and had the fresh smell of stones and minerals, but this liquid sparkled slightly in the sunlight, its surface an odd blue-black. It smelled of the sea.

Following her gut, she removed her wand from her belt and touched the water's surface with its tip.

A comforting sensation rolled up her arm and down her body, a feeling like someone had set a blanket on her shoulders or given her a thoughtful gift. Voices rose in her ears, whispers, a gentle singing.

"Set it to your forehead," the chorus of voices whispered.

Rhianne raised the wand and placed the end of the smooth branch between her eyes.

Bright, sparkling aquamarine and ruby shapes flooded her vision. Skeins of wool in every color of the rainbow threaded across her vision, and the comforting sensation that had touched her now lifted her to standing. She felt taller, stronger, more alive.

The world burst into noise again, wind in the palms, birds in the trees clicking and chirruping like they were asking her questions.

"Lyra's blood sings through your veins, new witch," the voices sang, clear and true. "Long asleep, your power now wakes. Defeat the old Matchweaver, the one known as Edwinde. She is chaos, a vortex, the winding abyss. Go and fight her darkness."

Tears burned Rhianne's eyes, and power hummed in her fingertips and in the center of her brow. Her vision remained colored with extra yellows and pinks, blues, and reds.

When she turned to face Werian, he dropped to one knee, his horned head bowed. Prisms of light danced off his hands and shoulders. Only now did she see his fae magic, the power he held. The plants near him glowed more brightly than the others.

"Goddess witch Rhianne," he said, his voice deep like thunder, "you bless us with your company. Allow me, Prince Werian of the Agate Court, to serve you."

Feeling like this was all a wondrous dream, she set a hand on his head. "Rise, my prince."

He stood, Brielle and Zahra at his back, grinning.

She took a breath as her vision returned to normal. "I am the Matchweaver."

CHAPTER 24

WERIAN

Werian leaned on the ship's smooth railing and gazed into the dark sky. "I like it. It's no *Nucklavee*, but still. It's a solid vessel."

His crew moved about the ship Zahra had kindly provided. The deck gleamed from a fresh scrubbing and the sails snapped pleasantly in the wind.

"Will you get another ship of your own?" Rhianne asked.

Every word they spoke was dulled with trepidation and laced with anxiety over what they would find in Lore. Neither of them had spoken of it again and the avoidance of the subject only proved their fear.

"Definitely. I'll use this one to sell the agate I have stashed in a chest near the palace, then purchase one of our own."

"Or you'll steal one from a deserving Wylfen crew."

"Exactly so." Wind filled the sails, and they were off, headed back to Lore, which meant it was time for...

Little John's shawm blew a deep, melodious tune into the air, and the crew gathered around a confused and absolutely adorable Rhianne.

Werian went to one knee and held out a ring with a sapphire that would dwarf every jewel at the Agate Court and beyond. "Will you marry me, fair witch goddess?"

He was surprised how nervous he felt, his stomach twisting and a bead of sweat forming on his brow.

Rhianne was a vision. They'd agree to no glamours aboard until they were in sight of the Sea's Claw, so her chestnut hair gleamed in the starlight and her eyes shone with their true light. She looked down at him, a smile on her pink lips.

"Answer me, you vile thing. I'm dying down here."

"Put him out of his misery!" Eamon shouted. He was only a bit angry when they'd come clean about the spell and the trousers.

Rhianne took the ring. Then she launched herself into Werian's arms, throwing him backward and landing on his chest. She kissed him soundly, and he held her tightly against his body, loving the soft feel of her curves and the heat of her embrace.

"We must stand up and dance now, my love, or this situation will become inappropriate."

She laughed, her swan throat bared to him, and he couldn't hold himself from nipping it with his teeth before they untangled themselves and joined in the dancing.

He spun her around as Little John played faster and faster. "If we live beyond the next several days, what do you say to an incredibly lavish and sparkling wedding at the fae court?"

She grinned and looked every inch a witch. "I'd love it. Will all those fine folk have to bow to me?"

"You are a demon, aren't you?" He smiled against her soft hair. "Yes, they most certainly will." And he would ask Aury to be there so his kin and kind could bow and beg forgiveness to her for what she'd suffered growing up at court. That apology was well overdue.

Rhianne kicked her foot to the side, drawing him into some sort of village reel.

"I haven't done this one. Mind my feet, woman."

She giggled and kicked again, and he made himself slow so she'd appear the quick one. Sometimes he wished he weren't fae and they were on equal playing fields physically.

"Can we marry here, on the ship?"

"You like me so much that you wish to wed me twice?"

"I do!"

"Well, you heard the lady, my merry band! Let us have a wedding!"

Beorn held up a long sash of dandelion yellow. "I bought this at the market. I can string it up on the forecastle!"

Eamon appeared from the cabins with an armload of lanterns. "We'll light them all."

And soon the deck was a flurry of movement, color and light springing up along the sail lines and railings. Little John was in close conversation with Rhianne.

"What are you two plotting?" Werian asked.

"It's different at sea—the ceremony, I mean. We're discussing what you have to promise to me in the vows," Rhianne said, eyebrow quirking upward.

"Oh, dear. I am in trouble."

"Stand here." Rhianne took him and placed him to Little John's right. She stood to his left.

"It's time!" John announced.

"Remember who pays you," Werian murmured.

John winked. John never winked. Werian was definitely in trouble.

The crew gathered around as the sails billowed and the candles in the lanterns flickered in a half circle around Werian and Rhianne.

"Do you, Rhianne of Tyreh, take this fae prince, Werian, to be your life love?"

"I do," she said.

"And do you, Werian of Illumahrah, take this witch-goddess, Rhianne, to be your life love?"

"I do."

"Do you, Prince Werian, promise to take Rhianne on at least one sea adventure each year?"

He felt himself smile. "Of course I do."

"And to give her a proper shoulder rub after a hard day matching all the couples in Lore?"

Rhianne fluttered her eyelashes.

"I'm being swindled right now, and I'm just letting it happen. Of course, yes, I do."

"Then you, Rhianne, do you promise to remind Werian he is not the Source's gift to all the world every now and then so his head doesn't grow so large as to require larger hats?"

Werian laughed.

"I do." Rhianne remained completely serious.

"I think..." John rubbed the back of his head. "I think that's it? I've only married one couple, and it was ages ago."

"What about the hand wrapping?" Werian eyed a rolled length of twine someone had set on a barrel at John's elbow.

"Yes! Right." He took one of Rhianne's hands and one of Werian's, then bound them with the twine.

Despite her bravado, Rhianne's hand trembled slightly. Werian longed to wrap her in his arms and take her below decks. John went on about the sea and the wind and something poetic focused on love, of course, but Werian couldn't be bothered. Rhianne stole every shred of his attention. The way she nibbled her bottom lip and how her multi-colored eyes caught every movement of the sails. If she had been a witch when they'd first met, or if he hadn't dreamt of her, he'd have guessed he was under a mighty spell. He longed to wake up every morning with her beside him, to help her grab this life and live it to its fullest.

Finally, John stopped droning on and it was time for the sealing kiss.

With his free arm, he pulled her close. His mouth hovered over hers. "I do love you, you know."

"Of course, you do." Her lips lifted at one side, then she kissed him, and he was well and truly lost forever.

CHAPTER 25
RHIANNE

Later in the night, Rhianne followed Werian into the captain's cabin, where lanterns hung from copper hooks. Light cascaded across the bed's gold-embroidered coverlet. Pomegranates and daggers made of red and silver threading ran all along the edges. There was a package tied with a bow on the bed as well.

"What's this?" A note sat folded on top.

"I was told a woman with red hair had it delivered right before we sailed." Werian removed her cloak, then his, and hung both garments by the door. Just that simple act gave Rhianne lovely shivers. He was her husband. Hers. It was astounding.

She took up the note and read it.

Don't let that uppity fae boss you about.
Take him by the horns.
-Brielle

Rhianne laughed.

"What is it?" Werian untied the lacing at the top of his tunic and pulled it off.

She took a deep, shuddering breath, her skin feeling hot. "I like Brielle. I'm shocked I do."

"Not all Wylfen are monsters, it seems."

"No." Rhianne set the note on the side table near a carved wooden box and a silver-backed, horsehair brush. She opened the package to find a diaphanous, floor-length gown with green ribbons around the waist. "Oh."

Werian came up behind her and made a noise against the back of her neck. His skin was hot on her back. He wasn't wearing a shirt. She glanced down to see the hemmed ends of his trousers at his calf and his bare feet. He made that sound again.

"Are you purring?"

He kissed the spot below her ear. "I will if you wear that."

She grinned and pointed toward the far corner of the cabin. "Only if you turn around while I manage it."

"But your new dress...you'll need assistance."

"Oh, yes. Impractical lacing. I hate fussy clothing."

But as Werian began unlacing the stomacher, part of the fine clothing he'd purchased at the market before sailing, her mind began to change. The feel of his fingers moving slowly across the cloth, just brushing her body beneath...well, it made breathing terribly difficult. His wicked grin, handsome fae horns, and gorgeous shoulders and chest didn't help matters.

"I need to sit down."

"Ah." He took her hand and gave her support as she

stepped backward and dropped onto the bed. "I did promise to bring you to your knees." His dark eyes glittered. "I suppose this will suffice. Weak in the knees, are you?" There was a flash of white as he smiled, showing his sharp fae incisors. "Shall I continue, or do you need a moment?"

She couldn't seem to talk. Finally, she managed a quiet, "Yes, please."

Going to his knees, he finished the unlacing, then removed the stomacher. His gaze roamed the lines of her exposed neck and collarbone. She couldn't lie to herself. She quite enjoyed the attention. His skin was smooth under her palms as she dragged her hands over his chest and flat stomach. He shivered and shut his eyes.

"Are my hands too cold?" she asked.

His throat moved as he chuckled. "It's not that. I promise you. You are perfection." He took her wrist to his lips and kissed her pounding pulse point, then reached behind her to untie the heavy skirts she wore over her shift. With a quick and graceful movement, he somehow moved her and slid her skirts off and to the floor.

Then with fae-speed, he grabbed her up and lay her on the bed. On his elbows, he held himself up and looked down at her, his lips parted and his eyes half-lidded. She wanted him closer but didn't know exactly what to do or how to do it. He brushed her hair away from her face with a soft touch, then placed kisses over her brow and down her throat. She reached up and ran a finger down one of his horns. He growled and buried his face in her neck, kissing her roughly and letting his weight settle onto her. Her body glowed with heat, and she hooked one of his legs with hers. His hand rushed up her side to settle over her ribs as he pulled her bottom lip into his mouth for a moment before kissing her slow and languorously.

"I might die," she whispered into his tousled hair.

He drew back, his cheeks flushed and his eyes glittering with the banked power of the fae. "You're joking, yes? I can leave you alone tonight. We have our entire lives."

Her stomach dropped, and she snaked her arms around his neck. "No! Never. I might burst into flames, but we will perish happy, I think."

He chuckled against her ear. "I would burn with you for as long as you let me," he whispered as he moved over her and laced his fingers in hers.

The night became a blur of pleasure and joy as she learned fae princes were talented in more than just wit and war.

CHAPTER 26
WERIAN

Werian wished they could remain on the ship in that cabin for an eternity. But they were quickly approaching the rocky coast of Lore, and it was time to use the wild magic his love had found. "Time to be heroes, darling."

Rhianne was a red-cheeked vision beside him. He hated to do it, but they needed to replace their glamours to ensure he could continue being Captain Shadowhood if they succeeded in their current endeavor.

"I quite like the idea of saving everyone," Rhianne said.

"Face me, please. We must become our other selves for the ride through the Sea's Claw to Illumahrah. Then we can shed the disguises and finish this."

"You realize I have absolutely no idea what to do." Rhianne tried for a joking tone, but worry pinched her pretty eyes.

Werian turned them gold and magicked her hair

straight and black. "We will figure it out, I'm certain. You will know what to do when the time comes."

DOCKING WENT WELL ONCE THE HARBOR MASTER LEFT off all the questions about the ship. It was far finer than anyone else's at the Sea's Claw, though truth be told, Werian longed for the *Nucklavee*. He missed its simple lines and the memories worn into its wood. Ah, but life went on.

The dockside stables showed no sign of evil. The autumn-dressed oaks still displayed their curled, brown leaves, and the sky was a bright blue.

With Rhianne packed up and situated on Storm, Werian mounted Moon and readied to ride.

Beorn bellowed from the roadside. "Captain!"

Werian kicked Moon to a trot and headed toward Beorn, Rhianne behind him. "What is it?"

"You have a message. Halig was holding it for us." He handed Werian a folded note. It was from Filip, his black Balaur seal showing the constellation of the minor god Rigel.

ATHELLORE HAS LOST HIS MIND. AURY ISN'T FAR BEHIND because he won't do a thing to even try to fight whatever the darkness is spreading over Lore.

IT'S SWALLOWED ALL THE LAND AROUND LORETON PALACE, and an odd ivy has sprung up along the roads, bridges, and even inside the palace here. We know it's the old Matchweaver, but we don't know what to do to fight this. My scouts say the darkness bleeds into Shadowhood's realm there in the east province as well.

PLEASE COME AS SOON AS YOU ARE ABLE WITH WHATEVER magic you have found. We need help. Queen Gwinnith is fading fast, and I think my man, Drago, is looking sickly too. I fear the worst, and I believe the evil is centered here.

FILIP

"OUR LOFTY FRIENDS REQUIRE US AT THEIR HOME, Merewyn of the Bones. I can fill you in on the details as we ride if you are up for the journey."

"Lead on, Captain." Her eyes were serious, and fear had drawn the flush from her cheeks. She touched the wand hidden beneath her dark green cloak, and he said a silent prayer to the Source that he would be an asset to her and to Lore in this next adventure.

ONCE THEY WERE ON THE KING'S ROAD, WERIAN PULLED back to ride side by side with Rhianne. He told her what Filip had written. "What do you think is the situation there?"

"Sounds like our king is rather bullheaded."

"He is a loathsome man."

"If our good princess hates him, he must be. Does he have any reason to allow the Matchweaver to destroy his land? It makes no sense. And I should call the old witch by her name, the name the spirits at the well told me. Edwinde. I am the Matchweaver, and I don't want to give the evil witch that title any longer."

"Done. She is Edwinde, and she is cursed and will suffer our wrath. But how do we fight that which we can't see?"

Rhianne just shook her head and nibbled her lip. "And Filip said one of his men as well as the queen are weakening and seem sick?"

"Aye."

"That could be coincidence. We know the land is going black. We know Edwinde is capable of such a thing because of what Princess Aurora saw in her visions when she fought her, yes?"

"Correct. Edwinde claimed if anyone struck out at her, the land would die." He and Rhianne had spoken at length about the vision. She'd wanted to gather every bit of information on the enemy as possible, smart woman that she was.

"All that's left is to witness the evil and see what we can make of it. How long will it take?"

"Two days from here at least unless Filip finds us with his dragon friend and gives us a quick conveyance to the palace."

"He had no idea when we'd arrive home from Khem."

"No, and who knows if the dragon can even fly at this point." Werian's stomach hollowed as they topped a hill. Blackened farmland stretched as far as the eye could see. "Where does such a large beast find food in times like this?"

Rhianne exhaled, her hands balling tightly on her reins.

"We must hurry, Werian, and hope our horses can manage the trip."

They rode hard and stopped only when the horses were frothing and heaving. He healed them as best he could. Rhianne watered the animals from Werian's stash of supplies, not trusting the rushing creeks with banks dark as pitch. It was a quiet, desperate trip, devoid of the happiness Werian had experienced with her on the ship.

At one stop, he looked into a farmer's pond near the roadside as Rhianne took a private moment in the bushes. Werian's face peered back at him from the water, black weeds hanging over his reflection like massive spider legs. Fear didn't suit him at all. He looked terrible when he scowled and far preferred his visage draped in a grin. He tried to muster a smile, but the effect was gruesome. Standing and shaking off the melancholy, he met Rhianne at Storm's side and gave her a hand up. She offered him her smile, which lifted his spirits. He just hoped her small shoulders could handle the weight of everyone's fate.

About halfway there, Werian glamoured himself, then they ventured into the Wrenlynn village inn.

"Why not glamour me as well?" Rhianne asked.

"You have to be yourself from here on out. The people must see you as their new Matchweaver. You'll give them hope."

"But what if they put together Shadowhood and Werian as both seen with me?"

"If my secret is found out, so be it. The kingdom is at stake. You are the priority."

They were welcomed into the inn by the keeper and his wife.

"Oh, Captain Shadowhood!" the keeper shouted, dragging Werian inside. "What a stroke of great luck to be the ones to help you on your way. Ruby!" The keeper put a hand to the side of his mouth. "That's my wife. Ruby, get him some ale! And some for his lady friend, too! You have saved so many from starvation, Captain. So many. We in the eastern province will never be able to thank you enough."

"I enjoy annoying the rich. It's quite fun."

The keeper laughed and steered him toward a high table near the crackling fire.

A woman with a generous bust—presumably Ruby—bustled out of the kitchen with two very large pints. Werian didn't realize how thirsty he was until she set the drinks in front of his nose. He held a chair out for Rhianne, and they sat to refresh themselves.

The keeper promptly said beside Werian, his gray eyebrows bunching. "Burktop has all gone down sick."

"Where's that?" Rhianne asked.

Ruby wiggled between her and Werian. "The next village down the road. Every last one of them laid up like they have the fever, though the travelers we've spoken to say those sick are simply overtired and have no fevers or other symptoms."

Rhianne tapped a finger on her pint's side. "It must be related to the darkness."

"It's awful!" the keeper said, shaking his head of curly, white hair. "Are you going to fix things, Captain Shadowhood? They say the Matchweaver has done this to punish us all."

A flush rose in Rhianne's cheeks, and Werian

recognized the light of righteous anger in her gorgeous eyes. "It's no punishment," she said. "The old witch is now only called Edwinde. She is no longer the Matchweaver. The ancient witches took that power from the evil crone and gave it to me."

"What's this?" Ruby stepped back, a hand on her bosom. "You?"

Rhianne nodded sagely and produced her wand.

"By Nix's fire..." Ruby exchanged shocked looks with her husband.

"She speaks the truth," Werian said, knowing his reputation would help Rhianne.

Ruby disappeared into the back, then returned with a plate of cheese and two chicken legs. "Please take this. And thank you for what you do for Lore."

Rhianne took a few coins from the small bag Werian had given her on the ship and pressed them into Ruby's hand. "It looks delicious."

"Did you know the captain hid his first take from the Fae Queen in the Byde River just past here?" The keeper leaned on the table and regarded Rhianne.

Had it been in the Byde? Werian shrugged. It might be true. He drank more of his ale but held off on the chicken and cheese, making sure Rhianne had her fill first.

"Mind if I tell the story?" the keeper asked.

"No, go on. I'm busy with my drink." Werian winked at Rhianne.

"I'd love to hear it," she said.

The keeper went on about the chest of spirit agate and the skull and arrow markings seen on its lid. "It was the first use of his symbol."

Ruby nodded enthusiastically. "Aye, but now it's hidden in every good household. Under tables..." She leaned and tapped the underside of the surface.

Werian and Rhianne bent to look. Sure enough, they'd put his marking there.

"It's on the threshold too. Outside. So if Shadowhood's men, oh, forgive me, if *Captain* Shadowhood's men come by, they'll know we can keep our mouths shut."

After two more stories, the keeper and his wife gave them their privacy in an upper room. An owl called outside, loud and lonesome.

Rhianne removed her cloak, then fell into bed. "I'm exhausted."

"I'll sleep on the floor. You sleep."

"Not a chance, my prince. Get yourself up here and keep me warm."

He bowed low and did as she bid.

In the darkness before dawn, she stirred, her body pressed to his. "I want to try something."

"Oh?"

She smacked his chest. "Not here. I mean I want to try a spell on the darkness and see what I can do now that I've been to the well."

"You should. Are you ready to rise?"

"I am."

They dressed and were off with wrapped hotcakes and skins of watered wine from the keeper and his wife before the dawn had fully chased away the night.

CHAPTER 27
RHIANNE

Rhianne waited until they were past the boundary markers of Wrenlynn to try her idea. Werian helped her from Storm's back. She hated that she needed the assistance, but her body wasn't used to so much riding, and every inch of her was sore.

"Care to tell me what you're thinking?" Werian took Storm's reins and held both horses.

He and the horses looked bright in the midst of the terrible darkness. The black ground made Rhianne's eyes ache. She couldn't help trying to see something, anything. Shifting her boots and trying to focus, she nodded. "I want to see what the stuff is made of."

"Knowing is half the battle, eh?"

"Exactly so." She held her wand away from her body, arm extended, and let the power within her rise and twist.

"Your magic has a scent now," Werian said quietly.

"Later, my prince. I'm focusing."

He chuckled but kept his chatter to himself. He could be so distracting with his looks and his voice and his adoration.

Her arm vibrated as the magic unspooled through her bones and blood, threads of power weaving their way into the wand, concentrating the energy. She pushed the power at one spot of the darkness beyond where Werian stood. "Reveal, unseal." Twisting the wand, she imagined the threads of her power tugging back the dark magic. "Show me what you hide inside."

But nothing happened. She poured more power into the spell, focusing on her will, on what she wanted. Sweat broke out across her forehead and dripped down her temples as she shook.

"Rhianne..." Werian's voice sounded far away.

But the darkness drank in her energy, sucking it from the wand, from her body, ignoring the spell's purpose entirely. The blackened tree beside the spot withered, branches cracking.

Werian was suddenly pulling her backward as the tree crashed to the ground, not a step from where she'd been standing. She let Werian hold her up, his strong arms a haven.

"Are you all right?" he whispered into her ear, his voice panicked.

"I...I think I am. But it took my magic. It drank up the spell like you did that ale."

He huffed an exasperated laugh. "You still feel your magic inside you though, yes? Please say yes."

She felt for that humming spark of power inside her

heart, and it answered her, heat rising and spreading briefly to her fingers and toes. "Yes. It's still there. I'm just tired."

"Ride with me. Moon can handle us both easily, and I'll take Storm's reins. Just until you're feeling stronger."

Grateful, she slumped against him as they cantered steadily down the road. She slept for a time, breathing in his Naroniti scent and reveling in the feel of his chest and arms like a castle wall around her, protecting her.

"Wake, my love. We have arrived at Loreton Palace."

Rhianne blinked and looked up to see Werian as himself, horns and smooth jaw and mischievous eyes. She kissed his chin. "Thank you."

"You two will need to hold off on the courting. I won't lie. It's grown fully terrible here, friends." Prince Filip of Balaur stood with a collection of servants, stable boys, and a few elven knights who must have been his men. One light-haired elven lord wore all black leathers and a scowl. He resembled Filip.

Werian helped Rhianne down, and she was happy to note she felt fine now, all that fatigue gone. She and Werian bowed low to Filip.

"Ah, enough of that. Come, let me introduce you to everyone." He pointed to a pale, elven knight wearing an eye patch much like the one Werian wore as Shadowhood. "This is Drago."

The knight bowed, but the movement was slow and less graceful than elves were known to be. "This place has grown steadily more depressing every day, Prince Werian.

I've finally escaped my sickbed, but I don't know how long I can handle this sad place! Please tell me you and your lovely lady are here to liven things up."

"That's exactly why we're here," Werian said.

Filip clapped a hand on the shoulder of the elven man who looked like him. Though Filip was dark-haired and this fellow was fair-haired, they shared the same strong cheekbones and the same set of the jaw. "This is my elder brother, Dorin, high prince of Balaur."

Werian and Rhianne bowed low to the next king of the mountain realm of Balaur.

"Greetings," Dorin said with a deep voice, his slanted eyebrows giving no emotion away. "It's a tragedy that we meet in such dire circumstances."

"And this is Costel," Filip said, pointing to a frizzy-haired, elven knight with a scroll under his arm. Costel grinned. He had a nice face. "Beside him," Filip added, "is Stefan."

The tall, slim-faced, elven lord bowed, twisting his hand in a flourish. "I'm the only one you should trust in this group, my lady."

Werian held Rhianne's hand. "Lady Rhianne of Tyreh is our new Matchweaver, chosen by the ancients and given full power at the old well of Khem."

Rhianne blushed under the shocked looks of so many handsome knights and princes. "I have come to root out the evil that has taken hold here. Although, I must be honest. I don't know where to start."

"Aury scried your moment at the well," Filip said. "She told us you were the new Matchweaver."

A woman with silver hair flew out of the palace's side

door, her face a storm. "Filip! I can't take it one more second. I'm going to freeze his lips shut and drown him in the river."

Filip grabbed the woman's hand and kissed it quickly. "And of course, this is our Princess Aurora."

Rhianne's mouth popped open, and she bowed low. The princess was so beautiful and a bit frightening too.

Aurora walked up to Werian and hugged him tightly. "Thank goddess Nix you're here. Tell me everything." Aurora gave Rhianne a kiss on the cheek, then looped her arm in Rhianne's and dragged both her and Werian toward the palace.

"You'll never tame that one, Filip!" Drago laughed, and Rhianne heard the sound of a punch and a huff, then more guffaws.

"Ignore them," Aurora said. "I want you to see the throne room. I think that's the center of the problems, and I just know the Matchweaver is behind this. It looks so much like what I saw in my vision."

"You mean Edwinde," Rhianne corrected, keeping her tone respectful. "I am the Matchweaver."

"Oh, yes! Of course. I'm so, so glad you're the new witch goddess. This old one needs to be taken down and soon before we're all dead. Did you see the circle under Drago's good eye? He's lost two stone in as many weeks."

Werian frowned. "That's horrid. And your mother?"

Aurora's lip curled. "Please call her the queen."

"The queen."

"She has taken to her bed. Haven't seen her in three days, but Alfred, that's our butler, assures me she is alive.

Athellore doesn't visit her chambers now. Normally, he has a private dinner with her at least once every seven days or so. He is not himself."

"How could he possibly be worse?" Werian asked.

"He released his guard," Aurora said, "sending every one of the good men packing. Then he hired a bunch of heartless fiends. They guard him now. They're the worst of the kingdom, drawn from the prisons. And it wasn't as if they were wrongfully imprisoned. These men are brutal."

An archway opened into a great room with towering ceilings, dark wood beams, and walls hung with richly colored tapestries. Dark ivy spiraled from cracks in the floor to crawl up the pillars at the sides of the room. Darkness cloaked the floor tiles like a thick mold and crept up the curtains over the other archways where the king's men stood on guard. Two thrones sat on a dais, but only one was occupied. More ivy grew up one side of the king's throne, sharp leaves twining around his wrist and pressing against the king's throat like a thief's dagger.

"Do not bother me, Daughter," King Athellore said, his voice a rasping whisper.

Aurora's nostrils flared. "But we have guests, dearest father. I'm sure you want to see if they can help us with the evil spreading in Lore."

His head turned like he was a marionette on strings. The moment his gaze met Rhianne's, she saw a flash of swirling green and black, then it was gone.

She stumbled back a step.

"Rhianne?" Werian caught her then helped her away from the throne room.

The two of them gathered in the corridor while Aurora argued with her father, the king.

"That isn't Athellore." Rhianne knew it in her bones. "The Matchweaver, I mean, Edwinde has taken hold of him. I saw..."

Werian smoothed her hair from her forehead. She hadn't realized she was perspiring. "Take your time. I'm listening."

"I saw the darkness and ivy. There's a taste on my tongue..." It was impossible to put into words, but the magic was Edwinde's.

"What do we do from here?"

"I don't know."

Aurora met them in the corridor, and Filip came quickly from the other side, concern and questions in their faces.

"Tell me what to do," Aurora said to Rhianne.

A princess was asking her what to do. Rhianne shut her eyes and put a hand over her stomach. Werian braced her back with his arm, and she felt his healing magic soaking into her body. Her muscles relaxed, and the heat in her head eased.

"Edwinde, the former Matchweaver, has control of the king," Rhianne whispered.

A decidedly evil grin stretched over Aurora's mouth. She spun and strode into the throne room, the rest of them following her.

"What's she doing?" Panic rose in Rhianne's throat. "If she attacks him, won't his men—"

Aurora raised her staff and thrust it at the king. Water soared from two large washing bowls at the end of the room, solidified into ice shards, and shot at the king's chest.

"Take her!" the king shouted.

The guards ran at Aurora, who seemed surprised. The king waved his fisted hand, and the ice shards smashed against the floor. A guard with beady eyes snatched Aurora's staff while the other took hold of her arm. Filip exploded into action, bumping Werian and Rhianne to the side. He shot forward with his elven sword and cut the beady-eyed guard down with one stroke. Aurora leapt for her staff and caught it as Filip fought the second guard. More guards were running at them as Werian pulled his sword and thrust into the fray.

What spell could Rhianne use? What would be the most help?

The king looked on, eyes narrowed and that same hand fisted around something.

Rhianne raised her wand and pointed at the king's curled fingers. "Release, unbind, reveal. Release, unbind, reveal." She was shaking as magic oozed from her wand too slowly. "Release, unbind, reveal!"

Her magic, pale and wispy, dragged across the king's hand. But he didn't open his fingers. Instead, he turned toward her and smiled.

A wave of nausea overwhelmed her, and she bent double, nearly dropping her wand. Where was this newfound power of hers? Edwinde must be suppressing it somehow. Forcing herself upright, Rhianne tried to raise her wand again.

Werian was fighting off two guards, his mouth in a grimace and his fae eyes flashing dangerously. Filip spun too quickly for Rhianne to see him clearly, then he beat back three more guards in Lore livery. Drago, Stefan, and Costel stood together as a ring of kingsmen descended on them. Filip's elder brother Dorin was a sight—golden haired, dressed in leathers as dark as night, and moving like sunlight on water as he struck down two guards with one slash, then turned to help Filip.

Where was Aurora?

A flash of green moved at the side of the room. There. Aurora was lashed to the floor in ivy, and darkness spread over her boots and up her legs.

"Halt!" Rhianne said, energy surging through her, heart pounding in her ears.

The darkness shivered and slowed its rise as Aurora struggled against a gag of ivy at her mouth and the dark greenery holding her hands against her body.

"Unspool, give way. I am the Matchweaver this day." Rhianne's body jolted as magic lunged out of her, into her wand, then shot out in Aurora's direction. Scarlet yarn spun from thin air and laced itself around the ivy strangling Aurora. With a tugging Rhianne felt in her navel, the wool tore at the ivy. Aurora's head, mouth, and right arm were freed. Aurora grabbed for her mage staff, but she choked, making a gagging sound, then fell quiet, the ivy reworking itself across her mouth and arm. Her eyes closed like she'd fallen to sleep.

"No!" Rhianne whipped her wand around in a slanting angle, and a hundred threads of scarlet burst from the air to grab the king.

The king stood and thrust his clenched fist in her direction.

Pain flared across her skull, and she dropped her wand, grasping for her hair, tugging at it. The world went gray. Her knees hit the floor, and the distant clang of swords echoed in her ears. Werian was shouting, but all she could focus on was the piercing, furious agony in her head.

CHAPTER 28
WERIAN

Werian snatched the wand, then grabbed Rhianne and carried her from the throne room. Those not tied in ivy and cloaked in darkness followed him. Fear was a monster clawing at his chest, riding his back, ripping his sense away.

"Dorin!" he shouted to the golden heir of Balaur, who walked by his side. "Can you ride?" The elven prince was bleeding freely from his shoulder. The scent of it was strong and sickening.

"I'm all right," Dorin said. "What is your plan?"

"What makes you think he has one?" Drago snapped and threw the main palace doors open.

They ran outside, where it was eerily empty of guards. Perhaps that was the lot of them inside, fighting for the foul king and his mind's captor.

"Because he moves like a man who knows his business," Dorin said.

"That's how he always acts." Drago shucked his eye

patch off, rubbed the scar over his temple and brow, then replaced it.

"We need horses and shovels," Werian said. "I do have a plan, Drago, and I'm inspired by your confidence in me."

Drago rolled his good eye as Dorin rushed into the stables and barked at the boys there to get four horses saddled. They seemed slow to act, their faces pale with fear. "Now, lads!" Dorin banged a fist against the frame, making the thatched roof shiver.

Drago ran to a supply shed past the stables and came out with three shovels.

Werian pressed a kiss on Rhianne's forehead. Her eyelids fluttered, then opened.

"My head..." She moaned and shut her eyes again.

Werian's world narrowed to her and her pain. He set a hand against her cheek and poured his magic into her, imagining the crisp mornings in the forest, the deep green of pines, the scent of moss and petal.

Rhianne looked at him and smiled, her color much better. "Thank you."

He handed her wand over. "We must hurry. I don't know what will happen to Aury and the rest. It might be too late already. But I do have an idea."

"I love your ideas," she said, her voice sadly weak.

Dorin approached with the horses, geldings all. Moon and Storm were surely resting.

Werian helped Rhianne onto a black mount, then climbed on a gray as a stable boy lashed a leather-wrapped shovel behind the saddle. Dorin tied his shovel securely, then swung a leg over a horse with four bright white socks, Drago likewise preparing.

The gray danced on the castle's cobblestones, and Werian whispered to the beast to soothe him. The group was mounted and alert. "Ready, all? We have a pirate stash to find."

"How in the name of Arcturus and Rigel is that going to help anyone?" Drago shouted as they galloped out of the castle walls.

"Have faith and stop your pestering, man!" Dorin called, his accented voice booming through the eerie silence.

"I second that!" Rhianne piped up.

WERIAN STOPPED THEM AT A CLUSTER OF LARGE OAK trees. They dismounted under the blackened limbs, Dorin looking up into the black leaves that hung like dead hands along the branches.

"Dig here." Werian started the hole himself. He and Little John had buried the chest of spirit agate what felt like ages ago.

Though Drago didn't have the bulk of Dorin, the fellow dug nearly as quickly. "What's down here, Prince? I'm through with your mysteries. My good friends are dead or dying back there."

"As are mine," Werian snapped. He glanced at Rhianne, who clenched her wand like someone might steal it. "You'll see, Lord Drago."

Dorin's shovel first hit the chest, and then it was quick work between the three of them. Good thing they were fae and elf and not weaker humans.

Werian hit the lock with a fist and broke it. He lifted

the lid and waved the glamour of the feigned amphorae away. Sparkling stones, sheared in halves, glittered like black diamonds.

Drago, Dorin, and Rhianne gasped.

"All the gods..." Drago leaned forward and whistled.

Werian took two large pieces and dashed them against one another.

"What are you doing?" Rhianne blinked at the beautiful mess on the ground.

The spirit agate had no effect on Edwinde's terrible darkness, but neither did the dark magic overtake the stones—or their own bodies, for that matter. Werian never would have stepped on the evil stuff without his boots though. It was obviously making people grow sick and die. Perhaps it was the time they were exposed added to their susceptibility and health...

He shivered and picked up the tiny bits of agate. "Rhianne, we'll tool these into your cloak, your belt, your hair..." He stepped closer to her. "We will dress you in power, darling, and then you'll return to fight the dark king and his spirit captor with us at your back."

"Oh!" The wind tossed Rhianne's hair. "The agate will increase my power if I wear it?"

Dorin almost smiled as he rubbed his chin. "It should work."

"It will work. It's my plan," Werian said, shaking his head. These elves...

Crouching, Drago studied one of the pieces that Werian had cracked. "How will we attach it?"

"That's where I come in!" Rhianne lifted her wand, pointed it at the shards around Drago's boots, then whispered something Werian couldn't quite hear. The bits of spirit agate shot at her cloak. Fine threads of scarlet appeared out of the air and sewed themselves around the stone, securing them to the woolen hem.

"See?" Werian crossed his arms. "My plans always work."

Rhianne smiled and began magically lifting more agate and stitching it to her belt with her power as a Matchweaver. "Magical thread is incredibly practical."

Werian touched her back. "And that suits you perfectly."

After they'd crushed and adhered as many pieces of spirit agate to Rhianne as possible, she stood back. "I want to try a spell and see how it feels."

"We don't have the time!" Drago leapt onto his horse. "Filip and Aury are dying back there. Come on!" He galloped off.

Rhianne nodded, looking a little ill, then let Werian help her onto her horse. She was quite heavier with all the stones. She looked like a legend on her horse, the sparkling black stitched into her braids, hanging from her neckline, threaded to her collar and around her fingers.

He touched her boot. "You can do this."

A raven's call echoed through the air.

Werian, heart in his mouth, glanced at her. Was it already too late? Rhianne swallowed and kicked her mount, trailing Dorin and his galloping horse.

Werian hurried to follow his witch to war.

CHAPTER 29
RHIANNE

Rhianne barely felt the added weight of the spirit agate stones, but their power infused her every thought with clarity. Her confidence soared, even though a part of her feared that was exactly how Edwinde would take advantage of her, by whirling past that confidence and striking to the heart.

The throne room was horrible. The only noises were the slithering of ivy across the jet-black floor, the wheezes of those encased in vines and cloaked in darkness, and the clicking of the king's tongue in a rhythm that pierced Rhianne's confidence like a series of arrowheads.

"Good," the king said. "You've returned. Let's finish this so I can drag all of Lore into the darkness its ungrateful inhabitants deserve."

Gripping her wand with a sweating hand, Rhianne tried to think of what to do. She'd forgotten everything. She couldn't think at all.

The king stood, his body moving unnaturally, his weight not truly on his feet. The effect dragged steel down Rhianne's spine. The king's voice rose. "I will revel in the last cries of the last death."

His fisted hand twitched, and a fallen sword flew from the ground toward Rhianne. She lifted her wand to cast a spell, to defend herself, but there was no time, no moment to think—

Werian leapt between the blade and her body.

A scream spilled from her mouth, wild and harsh, as the sword plunged into Werian's chest, the bloodied tip showing through the back of his clothing. With a guttural sort of gasp, he dropped to his knees, and with a burst of fae strength, he pulled the sword free. Blood flowed down his body.

No, this was impossible. Werian was the fae prince. Nigh on immortal. Hers forever. He couldn't die.

Hands and feet numb as rocks, Rhianne shuddered and raised her wand. Her vision blurred. "Bind and bind and bind and bind." Her mind seemed to tilt, her thoughts crashing against one another and the ivy and black-cloaked room going hazy. Magic curled from her wand as the guards and the king advanced on her.

The fight was frenetic. Drago and Costel dashed here and there, swords clashing with the king's men. Drago slashed at the nearest guard, missed, then struck the guard in the back. Frizzy, red hair plastered against his sweating forehead, Costel jabbed the tip of his sword into one burly knight, who spit blood. But there were more coming at them fast. Howling with rage, Prince Dorin fought with mind-boggling speed, cutting down two of the king's men with a high, spinning move before turning to parry a strike from another. He was as deadly as an electric storm cloud.

Werian coughed at Rhianne's feet. He looked up and smiled crookedly.

Her heart snapped her in two.

Then everything moved with the agonizing slog of a fever-slowed delirium, and she longed to fall down beside him, to help him somehow, but she had to try to fight. "You can't die."

"If you haven't noticed, I'm not very good at following orders, my gorgeous witch."

"Figure it out, Prince," she choked out as magic unspooled around her. Why wouldn't her power attack the king? Something held it at bay. Her fear?

"You get to save the day," Werian rasped. "At least let me go out like a fantastic hero." He tried to laugh, but his skin grayed, and his eyes closed.

Despair tore at her with jagged claws, and she glared at the king.

"You did this!" With every ounce of her strength, she pushed at her magic, willing it to wrap around King Athellore and his guards. Her mind trembled, every thought withering like leaves under a crippling frost. Why couldn't she think or act or fight? What was happening?

The king collapsed, and Rhianne's world went dark.

A twist of glowing ivy wove through the darkness.

"We will finish the prince now," a voice whispered in her head, "and then we will head to the ramparts to watch the world die."

The idea bled a pleasant feeling into Rhianne, but her stomach turned. Why was she fighting the voice? The voice was her, was them... No, that didn't make sense. She tried to touch her temples, to press against the odd feeling, but her hands refused to move.

"Point the wand at the fae prince," the voice said, the words like a powerful ale that made her unsteady.

Her hand obeyed her this time, raising the magical weapon and looking down at the bleeding prince. She knew him, didn't she? Cold shot through her body. She did! She—

"Shhhhh," the voice whispered.

Rhianne's panic settled into some dark, dark corner of her mind even as this prince spoke to her, his words too quiet to hear. "What was that?" she asked him, her own words garbled.

"The crone has taken your mind, my love," the prince gasped out, a black lock of hair subtly touched by purple hanging over his face. He was so beautiful with his soft lips canted in a tender grin and his powerful-looking body, his arms and legs like roots of a strong tree... It was so sad he was dying. "Call her...by her name," he said. "You know her. Expel her. You can do this." The tip of one of his ram-like horns had been knocked off. He coughed, and his fine eyes closed again as the voice's ivy crawled over his stomach.

"He is mad," the voice said inside Rhianne's head. "Put him out of his misery. It's a mercy. Release your magic to me. To us. For us."

The voice was right. He did seem near to death and was babbling. It was best to let him die. Of course, it was. The voice knew all things.

Magic rose strong and shimmering in Rhianne's blood, and scarlet threads slithered from the air around her to wrap the prince's neck tightly. It would be quick and merciful. The voice knew best.

CHAPTER 30
WERIAN

As the woolen threads crisscrossed Werian's throat, his body blazed with pain, his energy nearly spent. He hadn't planned to go like this. A shame, he thought sadly. And Rhianne, her eyes gone a sickly green, stood over him, wand poised to kill. The old Matchweaver possessed her—it was clear in the ill-fated color marring the rainbow hue of her eyes, that slack look to her face...

He was dying.

"Name," he managed to croak. "Call her name."

The Matchweaver's name—the one Rhianne had shared with him after she'd learned it at the well—it wouldn't come to mind. Blood loss, lack of air, or magic, he wasn't sure which was fighting him there.

Whatever it was, it was winning handily, curse it all.

His life had been on the path to being absolutely stuffed with fantastic experiences, but now it would be taken by the very woman who sparked the most happiness in him. At least his death was gorgeously tragic. No dull falling to sleep as an old fae to wake in the next life. No, he had made a sacrifice.

"Love you, little fox," he whispered, watching Rhianne's dark magic curl from her wand like the very spirit of death come to call.

"What name?" she asked, her lip trembling. She blinked and shuddered.

She was fighting back.

What was the cursed witch's name? Gods above, why couldn't he think or speak properly? His arms wouldn't even move, and he could barely speak. "Crone's name. You know it."

His eyelids were so heavy. His heart beat sluggishly in his chest.

"I'll miss you," he tried to say as he finally let go.

CHAPTER 31
RHIANNE

Rhianne watched the prince's body relax. No. She didn't want to see him dead. She undid the woolen magic laced around his throat.

Why didn't she want him to die?

A desperate fear ran across her foggy mind and made her taste metal on her tongue. Two elves—one with an eyepatch and the other very tall and golden-haired—fought the king's guards, but thankfully, they were losing. All would be quiet and so very dark soon.

"All will be just as it should. They need this," the voice said.

Rhianne wanted to listen to the voice and be comforted, but fear shook her thoughts and heart, gripping both in cold hands. What had the prince said before he gave in to death? Her name. The crone's name.

"No. Stop," the voice said.

"Are you the crone?" Rhianne asked the voice aloud

even though the voice was inside her, and indeed was a part of her own self.

The voice sounded angry. The fear in Rhianne liked it. She felt herself smile against the pull of the voice.

"Do I know you?" Rhianne asked.

The clanging of swords was muffled as the men and elves fought on. The fae prince at her feet lay completely still.

"Shhhh." The voice made Rhianne start toward the elven warrior with the eye patch. "Kill them. Send them to sleep with their friend, the prince. It is a kindness. I know what comes next in this kingdom. They will not wish to see that. Even now, the people of Lore die of the spreading night. It is as it must be."

Lore? Rhianne blinked, her fear shaking her mind again. That was where she lived. In the kingdom of Lore. She'd left her village not so long ago... Why had she left?

To find the Matchweaver.

"No! Listen!" the voice called out, the harsh sound painful in Rhianne's temples.

The Matchweaver.

Truth swept through the voice's shouting. It all came back at once. The ancients. Her wand.

"Werian!" Rhianne's heart shivered, and she whirled to see him dead on the ground. "No! Werian!" Had she done this? She dropped her wand and fell to the floor near Werian's feet.

"How could you?" she shouted to the voice still writhing in her head. She had thought the voice was a friend, was her soul, but now— "You hurt him, the man of my heart..."

"No," the voice cooed. "He did it himself. Sacrifice. Now, lift that wand and end those men. I want to see you do it, usurper!"

Rhianne's body obeyed the voice, and she stood, feeling too light. She grabbed her wand and lifted it high above her head, magic swirling and sparkling along the spirit agate stitched to her clothing, dark and light around her like a storm of her magic and the voice's.

Who was the voice?

She tried to look back at Werian. What had he said?

Name. Her name.

The memory of the ancients' calming, powerful whispers drowned out the crone's voice.

"Edwinde!" Rhianne shouted. Her body thrashed, torn between two masters. "Edwinde, I name you, and I expel you!"

Sparkling blue flecks of magic burst from Rhianne's wand to coil around her head and hands. The spot between her brows burned like a match flickering against her skin.

There was a scream. Her scream and Edwinde's.

The throne room burst into bright, white light. Rhianne was lifted into the air. Wincing against the light, she curled in on herself, then her limbs were thrust outward, and her boots hit the floor. She was upright and gasping.

The voice was gone, and her mind was quiet. The old witch's presence had fled the room, perhaps the world? She could only hope.

Like waking from a dream, Rhianne shook herself. Shaking and sweating, she pointed her wand at the king's men. Wool flew through the air to bind their arms to their sides, swords falling. Drago and Costel whooped a cheer, and Dorin exhaled loudly, his eyes going to his younger brother Filip.

But Rhianne could only think of Werian.

She went to her knees by his side and set the wand against his wound. He was so pale.

"A sacrifice made in my name," she whispered as rose-pink magic flowed into his body. "A second chance with you I claim."

The spirit agate on her sleeves and the hem of her cloak flashed brightly, and powerful magic threaded through her chest and arm, then into the bleeding gash left by the sword. It had to work. Warm tears ran down her cheeks to drop onto his vest. She didn't want to disturb the fabric torn around the wound in case it only made things worse.

Werian's eyes fluttered open. "Eh, that rhymed. You're improving, fox."

She let out a surprised laugh, her tears flowing harder.

"Please!" Dorin called out, his voice deep and laced with agony.

Rhianne helped Werian stand, then she made a great circle with her wand. "Dispel the dark bindings, the foul spells of Edwinde's wicked workings!"

The magicked ivy holding Aurora, Filip, and the other elven warriors who'd been taken down exploded into clouds of bright purple, then dissipated across the throne room. The darkness sped into the corners like it feared Rhianne's anger.

Dorin helped Filip to stand, then hugged his brother tightly. Stefan, now free, joined Costel and Drago in leaping onto Dorin and Filip until the lot of them fell into a laughing heap. Aurora rolled her eyes, but her grin gave away her true feelings.

"To the walls, if you please, Matchweaver," Aurora said to Rhianne. "We must see what you can do for the rest of our kingdom."

"Of course!" Rhianne hurried off, her hands trembling but her legs steady. The spirit agate's power flooded her with a strength she'd never felt before now.

"You're nearly as fast as I am!" Werian said, handily catching up as they rounded a corner.

The front doors gaped open, and they ran hard across the courtyard, heading for the staircase to the guard's tower at the front gate.

At the top, Rhianne looked out across the Silver River, the fields, the distant forests. The deadly magic of Edwinde was retreating, the color of the land returning bit by bit. It seemed by expelling Edwinde from her mind, Rhianne had also thrown the evil witch from the land.

"It looks like a painter's work." Awe held her still.

The trees' autumn oranges, browns, yellows, and reds rose slowly, replacing the darkness. Sunlight glittered along the water, and even the stones under Rhianne's hand regained their steely hue. Werian jumped a little, looking at his boots as dark, magicked ivy fled past him and Rhianne only to disappear in a cloud of purple.

Lore regained its bright colors—autumn's raiment—and Rhianne set her head on Werian's shoulder. He tugged her sleeve and nodded to the courtyard behind them.

She turned to see Princess Aurora, Prince Filip, King Athellore, Queen Gwinnith, and all the rest bowing low.

"We thank you, Matchweaver," the king said, his voice rough.

"I'll be sure no one mistreats you like they did your predecessor," Aurora said, giving her father a pointed look.

Werian murmured quiet agreement as he ran a hand along Rhianne's back. She swallowed, now longing to leave all of this and revel in the fact that her fae prince was alive. He'd said he wanted to be wed at his court so his mother would have to recognize her as his mate and so Aurora could have a fine apology from the fae for the terrible childhood she'd experienced with them. Perhaps now was the time to organize that. It wasn't every day she had the attention of every royal in Lore.

"I hold no ill will against anyone," she said. "But I do have one request."

Filip took Aurora's hand in his, then met Rhianne's gaze, his gray eyes flashing. "Name it, and it is yours."

Aurora nodded.

"Prince Werian and I are to be wed at the Agate Court in one week's time. I request the presence of Princess Aurora and Prince Filip, and whoever else wishes to attend."

Werian kissed her temple. "Well done, fox." His hand slid lower on her back.

"Agreed!" Aurora called up, her lovely face radiant.

Rhianne curtseyed, Werian bowed, and all was well with the world.

CHAPTER 32
WERIAN

Werian looked in the mirror to ensure his cloak draped perfectly over one shoulder. The fine, velvet cloak had a dark green underside with a hidden bow, arrow, and skull embroidered in the inner pocket. He enjoyed knowing the trappings of his second personality would be right under the Fae Queen's arrogant nose at the wedding.

He eyed his new servant. "You look so familiar," he joked.

Little John smiled and adjusted his steel-gray and black brocade tunic. "Except your friend dresses more like a sloth turned into a man, aye?"

Laughing, Werian nodded and checked Little John's glamoured beard and eyes. "Comfort seems to be his first priority."

"I doubt that. He'd not work for you if he valued an easy life."

"Truly? I think a dull life would be the most uncomfortable lifestyle of all."

"So you're saying life without Prince Werian must be dull."

"You said it." Werian finished brushing his hair artfully around his horns, then strode out of the room.

The great hall was festooned in satiny, black banners, sheaves of wheat, and hundreds of pillar candles that gave off the lovely scent of beeswax and lavender. Long, velvet panels displayed the Agate Court livery—the sacred oak on a field of black—above the dais.

As Little John stepped away to allow Werian to make his entrance, the gathered crowd hushed and moved to the sides of the room.

Aury, water mage staff in hand, stood near the front with Filip, Costel, Drago, Stefan, and Dorin. He gave them a smile as he walked in, head held high. His new boots clicked on the mosaic tiles, and the sunset song of the birds in the courtyard carried through the open door.

At the dais steps, he stopped and waited for his mother to arrive. "The hag is late on purpose," he whispered to Aury. "She will pay though, don't you worry. She will pay."

"I can't wait to see it." Aury looked down her nose at the fae nearby, and Werian guessed she was thinking of those like that awful Bathilda who'd treated her poorly during her childhood here.

Werian's jaw tightened as his mother, the Fae Queen, strolled in wearing a luminous gown the color of the moon. She inclined her head to King Athellore and Queen Gwinnith. Werian hadn't realized they were here, blocked as they were by a monstrous floral arrangement.

The Fae Queen stopped at the edge of the dais, and Werian gave her a shallow bow. "Mother, dear, you forgot to bow to Princess Aurora and Prince Filip. I do believe you owe the princess a long-overdue apology."

Her nostrils flared and color rose in her cheeks as she looked for some excuse to put this off yet again.

"Ah, ah, ah," he said sharply, "there is no escape for you here. Bow, you monster, or you'll never see the heirs born of my union."

She didn't care for children, Werian knew that well. But she did care for continuing her line through her son. And so it was pride, not heart, that bent her into a curtsey before Aury and Filip.

Aury grinned like a demon, and Werian fought a laugh.

"Apologies, Princess Aurora," his mother said snidely, "for housing and feeding and tutoring you your entire childhood. I suppose my best efforts were not enough for one as high as yourself."

Werian shot forward. "That is not an apology. This is your last chance," he whispered.

Filip's hand had strayed to his axe, and the spark of a warrior's hunger flashed in his eyes. Werian was glad Aury had such a partner in life.

"Fine," the Fae Queen snapped. She lowered herself further into the curtsey. "Forgive me for permitting the snide remarks, strikes, and poor treatment my court cast upon you as a child. I will see them punished, each and every one."

"Oh, no," Aury said, her smile reptilian. "Your own punishment is more than enough to suffice. I appreciate your offer to kiss my house ring and beg for your life."

Werian coughed, shocked and grandly pleased at Aury's fire. "What a merciful ruler we will have in Princess Aurora."

His mother swallowed, her mouth pinched tightly and her hands fisted in her gown. She parted her lips to say something but seemed to think better of it. She kissed Aury's Lore ring. "Please spare my life despite my wrongdoing, Princess."

Aury gazed over the gathered fae court, and Werian glared, daring any one of them to do a single thing out of line. He would happily join Filip in backing her up. Bathilda seemed specifically partial to staring at the wall. Werian rubbed his hands together. Time for a bit of pre-wedding fun.

"Bathilda! What a lovely suggestion!" Werian said.

Her head whipped around, her eyes wide. "What?" she asked, her voice harsh amid the beauty of the room.

"You are such a kind lady to offer to wash down Princess Aurora's new palfrey every time she visits in penance for your ignorant cruelties of the past."

Bathilda frowned and shook with rage, but she curtseyed to him and then to Aury. "My pleasure."

"Oh, no," Aury said. "She's not getting anywhere near my animals. You can muck the stalls under supervision. Auntie," she said to the Fae Queen, "I'm sure you'd be willing to supervise, yes? After dining on the bread made from Lore wheat and the wine crafted from Lore grapes?"

Werian was overjoyed to watch his evil mother set a hand against a pillar to keep herself upright. Such a blow to her massive ego.

"Of course, your majesty," the Fae Queen whispered.

The court began murmuring, and all heads turned to see Rhianne walking into the hall.

Werian's heart tried to fly out of his chest. She was an absolute vision. Swathed in green, black, and gold, her dark tresses braided through a twisting fae crown—well, she quite literally stole his breath. An emerald veil like spider's silk draped from the top of her head over her shoulders and floated all the way to the floor. Golden lacing ran up the side of Rhianne's gown, drawing it in at her small waist and showing off her female shape. Her cherry lips lifted into an impish grin. The brat knew exactly what she was doing to him. By the light of the god Arcturus, he loved her.

She joined him on the dais, where they stood in a circle of spirit agate.

But the Fae Queen stepped forward. "I take issue with this proposed marriage as is my right as fae royalty."

Werian squeezed his eyes shut, fury burning a trail from his heart to his foul mother's mouth. He opened his eyes to see Rhianne not sad or cowering but lifting her wand.

"What is your issue?" Werian said through gritted teeth, quoting the old words taught to him during tutoring as a youth. He wanted their marriage binding in his kingdom, but how could he circumvent this without bloodshed?

"Rhianne of Tyreh is not powerful enough to be a royal fae's mate. She has but a shadow of the power the former Matchweaver held, and it will not be enough to offset her lack of fae blood."

Rhianne began whispering under her thin, green veil, her wand raised.

The room went dark.

Every candle snuffed and smoking.

Thunder growled and lightning cracked, illuminating Rhianne's partially shrouded glare and the Fae Queen's blinking eyes.

Someone gasped. Above the gathered guests, a gryphon —scarlet wool eyes, body of black and swirling smoke— hovered and shrieked. The magical creature reached smoky, lightning-filled talons toward Werian's mother. The Fae Queen crumbled, covering her face and calling for help.

Werian wished they hadn't released the court painter. A permanent image of this moment would have been a treasure.

Rhianne quieted the magicked thunder and stilled the gryphon with a flick of the wrist. "I'm sorry, Fae Queen. What were you saying?"

Oh, gods and goddesses, he loved it when she didn't play fair. He couldn't stop smiling.

The Queen rose and dusted herself off even as she kept an eye on the hovering gryphon and the silent lightning. "Nothing, Matchweaver. Nothing at all. Carry on," she hissed.

Rhianne turned to face Werian, her smile bright behind her green veil. "Shall we?"

He glanced at the gryphon and the lightning that lit the room. "Perhaps without the menacing groomsman and his stormy ambiance?"

She laughed and twisted her wand, whispering something. The storm and creature disappeared, and every candle flickered back to life.

He raised her veil, then took her hand and faced the court. "I, Prince Werian of the Agate Court, take you, Rhianne the Matchweaver, to be my eternal mate. My body, blood, and bone are yours to break and bind."

Her cheeks flushed like ripe apples. "I, Rhianne the Matchweaver, take you, Prince Werian of the Agate Court, to be my eternal mate. My body, blood, and bone are yours to break and bind."

As was fae custom, Werian set his mouth against her ear and whispered his true name. "Kāttin Mantiram. Magic of the forest."

She inhaled, her chest rising. "Thank you." Her serious eyes told him she appreciated the power he'd given to her.

Candlelight danced over her face, and he kissed her soundly. Her body gave slightly under the crush of his hold, and she felt like a dream against him. The court erupted in applause, Little John—still glamoured and standing in the corner—the loudest of them all.

Werian broke away reluctantly and lifted an expectant eyebrow at his mother, then at Athellore and Gwinnith, who stood barely clapping.

The human king and queen gave Rhianne a respectful nod as was custom at a royal fae wedding, then the Fae Queen slowly touched her forehead and lowered her chin.

Little John elbowed the lead piper, and music careened into the room, breaking through the tension with wild song. Werian bowed deeply to Rhianne, who took his hand. They led the dancing, spinning and jumping to the quick melody. Circles of fae and the humans of the Lore court surrounded the newly wedded couple, hands clapping and shoes clicking on the colored tiles of the hall's fine floor. Werian's wild cousin, Wynflaed, wove through the dancers with silver-haired Isen, only slightly wicked smiles on their faces. Rhianne's hair came loose around her shoulders, tangling with her emerald veil, and Werian took her hands again, pulling her close, reveling in the feel of her warm, dewy skin.

Filip danced with Aury, his elven movements as graceful as a fae's, while his brother Dorin danced with a flaxen-haired fae girl Werian had seen training horses now and again. Drago, Stefan, and Costel stood at the side of the room, daring Bathilda and a human male to match them drink for drink. Faery wine was not the same as elven; he hoped they knew. If not, they'd be rather surprised at how lost they were by midnight, following mysterious lights in the enchanted Forest of Illumahrah or accidentally promised to a fae for a year.

"Careful of that wine," Rhianne called out over the heads of a dozen wild-eyed courtiers.

Drago lifted his drinking horn and winked.

Rhianne bit her bottom lip. "Do you think they're all right left alone with your kind?"

"They're elven warriors. I'd say they can handle themselves." He wrapped Rhianne in one arm and set his lips on her ear. "You look absolutely delicious, my lovely mate."

She gazed up at him with a fantastic look of adoration he had to admit he loved. "The feeling is mutual, my prince."

Nipping her neck, he spun her around. "I'm more than ready to be done with the dancing." Keeping her fingers laced in his, he extended his arm and flung her outward in a fast spin.

"But you're so good at it."

"I'm better at other things."

She swallowed and blushed furiously. The crowd's circles broke into a chaotic mess of wild dancing, the pipers playing faster and faster. Yes, the party would be just fine without them. It was time for dessert.

Victory giving his feet wings, Werian led Rhianne out of the room toward his bedchamber. She tugged at his arm under the fluttering of the small gold and green ribbons released by servants from the high beams.

"So am I a princess or a fae princess now? How does that work?"

He ran light fingers over the back of her hand as the darkness and quiet of the corridor welcomed them. "You choose. That is how it works. You are the mistress of your own destiny."

She grinned, her dimples showing. "Well, that's a change I welcome. I think Matchweaver is title enough. I don't feel like a princess. I didn't even know which fork to use at last night's feast."

"I'll teach you if you want me to." He opened his bedchamber door. Little John had lit all the candles on the hearth, the windowsills, and on the tables beside the wide bed. A strong fire leapt in the hearth. He spun Rhianne around until he held her tightly, her breath catching in her throat. "I will happily tutor you in any subject your heart desires to understand."

She set her lips against his neck, her breath warm. "Like how to make you purr?"

He laughed, his body as hot as the fire. "Gods, yes, darling. Though you don't need the instruction." Gathering her into his arms, he brought her to the bed, where he began untying the lacing that ran down the right side of her gown.

Her fingers twisted in his hair as he made quick work of the dress. "What happens if I say your true name?"

"With the magic you have, I don't know. It's possible you would kill me as soon as you finish saying it."

She shot up and nearly caught herself on his horns. "Werian." Her hands cupped his face, her gaze darting from his eyes to his cheeks and chin. "Why did you tell me? What if an enemy takes the name from my mind? We both saw what Edwinde is capable of."

"Was capable of. I do think she was an exception in the world of magic."

Rhianne set her forehead against his. "If anyone ever takes my mind again..."

"It won't happen. You are unbeatable, my glorious witch-goddess." He kissed her and kissed her until she finally smiled and seemed to forget her fears.

CHAPTER 33
RHIANNE

Lying on the massive bed in Werian's chambers, Rhianne held her breath as Werian propped himself on an elbow and slowly drew her gown from her shoulder using his teeth. A lovely shiver danced through her as he looked up at her, his eyes delightfully wicked and his horns reflecting the golden candlelight.

"You should have to take your shirt off first," she said. "It's only fair."

His mouth quirked up to one side, and he sat up. "So you want me to remove my shirt for fairness' sake. That's your only reason." He took his crown and hers and set them on the nightstand beside her wand.

"Of course."

"Hmm." He cocked one black eyebrow as he unbuttoned his vest. Something about his fingers on the agate buttons made her feel too warm, as if the stones' power was increasing his ability to attract her. With the vest thrown to the floor, he lifted the ends of his undershirt to reveal his muscled, flat stomach and trim waist. His hipbones showed above his belt and the embroidered waistline of his trousers. Her hands moved toward him like they had a mind of their own, like they were eager to explore every inch of him. She curled her fingers to keep from grabbing him.

He tossed his undershirt across the bed with a flourish that tousled his hair. "Why are you holding back, my darling? You can do absolutely anything you like." On his knees, he spread his arms wide, showing off his chest and the ropes of muscle. "My gift to you is me."

"You're so humble."

"I think we've established I don't even comprehend the term."

She laughed as he fell on her like a predator on prey, his kisses preceding quiet growls and his hand splayed over her back, urging her close, closer. Her fingers traced the lines of his shoulders and sides, of a hipbone. She couldn't get enough of the texture of his fae skin. The heat of it and the way it seemed to glow when they were together like this made her head spin like she'd had a powerful drink.

She hooked her fingers into the waistline of his trousers and pulled him against her. "You're still wearing your dagger."

"I want to make a joke." He leaned over, unbuckled the entire belt, then let it drop. "My amazing self-discipline is keeping my tongue in check."

"That's my duty, Prince Werian."

Rhianne brought her mouth to his, in awe that she had this fae warrior prince in her arms, this man who had fought for her, battled beside her, believed in her every step of her way to becoming the Matchweaver. The sweep of his tongue across hers sent a surge of need through her body. She felt as if the blood in her veins was waking up and didn't quite know where to flow. She was hot and tingling all over, and the feel of him shifting over her was too much to bear without sighing.

Then she remembered their first day together and his reaction to her touching his horns. She ran one fingertip along the curve of his left horn. His hips bucked, and he inhaled sharply as he drew back. His eyes flashed open. He fixed a dangerous look on her. A thrill crashed across her belly and sent her heart into a frenetic rhythm. He wrapped his arms tightly around her, one hand gripping her hair lightly. A staccato sound echoed from the depths of his throat—a purr.

"Victory," she murmured as he flipped them over so she sat atop him.

"I'm aflame, goddess of mine, and make no mistake. You've fully done it now." He locked gazes with her once more, a question in his eyes, a request.

Her lips brushed his. "I'm quite happy, I promise you. Carry on."

He smiled against her mouth and set to kissing her up and down until she was near to fainting even though she'd never been the fainting sort. She grabbed his horns and drew his head back, exposing his throat.

"My turn." She ravaged his neck and chest with teeth and tongue and lips, adoring the feel of him beneath her.

"Release me," he whispered, a grin on his fine, fine mouth and the dimple in his chin and cheek showing.

She did, and suddenly she was against the wall, held up

by his body, his arms. The velvet draping over the stained-glass windows dropped to the floor beside them. Rhianne laced her legs around his waist and savored the feel of his hands on her and his intoxicating fae scent.

Here was the love of her life, a dangerous, royal, fae warrior who had a double life as a pirate. She never could've planned a more wonderful match, a more adventurous path for her life. With a whisper of gratitude to the Source, to the ancients, she gave way to being utterly and completely smitten with her enchanting fae prince.

Love was definitely worth the risk.

EPILOGUE
RHIANNE

In the candlelight of the dining table at the Matchweaver's castle, Rhianne finished her goblet of red wine and ate the last bite of brown bread with goat cheese and venison sausage. "What a fine dinner, Nor. Thank you very much."

Nor glowed as she motioned to the other women to clear the trenchers and bowls. "I only recently began cooking for the castle. Our head cook decided to leave after you cleared old Edwinde out."

"I can't believe she had a name," one of the serving women said, laughing. "I thought she was too high for a name."

Across the table from Rhianne, Werian grinned and nodded understandingly as he sipped from his goblet.

"The cook didn't leave because she was angry, did she?" Rhianne asked.

"No," Nor said, "she was too afraid of Edwinde to ask permission to go."

"Glad I could help." Catching up with Nor and filling her in on all the developments in person—of course she'd sent a letter earlier before the wedding—had been lovely, but now it was time to figure out what was next. She pushed away from the table and wiped her mouth on her napkin. "I need to learn to use the Mageloom. How many women are waiting to hear about their matches? You said you were housing them for the time being, yes?"

"Five women are here. They're working about the grounds just now with the others. I'll send for them when you are ready, Matchweaver."

"Please call me Rhianne."

"I don't know..."

"At least when it's just us. I can't handle standing on ceremony every second. And I only have a few friends. You're one of them. My friends must call me by name when we are visiting."

A wide smile stretched Nor's lips. "Fine then, Rhianne. I'll fetch the women and meet you at the Mageloom when the candles show an hour past."

"You're my steward here, Nor. You should have someone else doing the fetching." Rhianne squeezed her friend's hand in thanks, and Nor curtseyed.

Werian opened the side door for the serving women who held the trays of dirtied bowls, then caught up with Rhianne as she left the dining hall. She swung open the narrow, oaken door that protected the corridor and walked into the dark.

"Such an interesting castle this is." Werian's voice echoed off the walls of the tight space as they strolled toward the great hall where the Mageloom rested. "This secured second passageway, for instance."

"It's practical. The focus in this estate isn't feasting or holding grand events for nobles. The loom is the center of activity, and so keeping it in the great hall and placing the dining in the smaller chamber makes sense. As does this private entrance to the great hall." Candlelight drifted from the cracks in the doors at either end of the corridor.

"You say *practical* like others say *silk*," Werian said, teasingly.

"Like you say *silk*, you mean, you spoiled prince, you."

He grabbed her around the waist and set her against the wall, his mouth below her ear. "I am spoiled indeed."

Trailing open-mouthed kisses down her neck, he held her close, his large hands gentle despite his strength. His horns knocked the wall lightly, and sparks of heat cascaded through her body. He angled his mouth over hers and tortured her with shallow kisses that just barely brushed her lips. One hand slid down her leg to hook under her knee. He almost leaned against her but not quite. Her whole body ached.

"Werian..."

"Yes, my fox?" he whispered into her ear.

"Please."

"In the corridor?" His eyes seemed to flash in the near dark.

"I'm mistress here, am I not?"

He threw his head back and laughed joyfully.

Rhianne took her sweet time heading to the Mageloom.

. . .

THE MAGELOOM WAS EXACTLY AS RHIANNE REMEMBERED it. Lit by the sconces set into the walls, wool in every color of the rainbow ran the length of the black frame. Magic tingled against her witch senses, the power of the loom strong enough to affect her before she'd even picked up the shuttle. A new stool had been set where Edwinde's willow chair had once been, and someone had fixed the broken, colored windows.

Werian leaned against the frame of the corridor's entrance, watching her with a satisfied grin on his lovely mouth.

Rhianne sat and began to weave. With the faint echo of the ancients' whispering in her ears, she imagined the women of the Sea's Claw, the ones who had stared at the ship as they'd docked, excited to watch the sails in the wind. But the recent memory faded, and instead she saw herself on the parapet at Loreton Palace. She watched a watery version of herself cast the darkness from the kingdom, but in this vision, her magic was visible—scarlet and threading through the countryside to touch villagers and farmers, travelers and merchants, nobles and poor alike. The vision expanded to show all of Lore, or at least, that was what she assumed the loom was showing her. Scarlet Matchweaver power stitched its way from border to border, leaving... What? What was this? A cloud of sorts hovered over more populated areas, but what did it symbolize?

"You've given them a thimble-full of our power," the ancients whispered.

Rhianne's hands stilled on the shuttle, her fingers on the soft wool. "Did I make a mistake?"

"They will see their fated love in their dreams, most of them," the voices said, echoing and distant and at the same time so close to her ear. "Some will still come here, to the loom. But they will read their own fate there with the measure of magic you've given them."

A light glittered inside Rhianne. "They don't really need me here, then?"

"You are free, Matchweaver. Because of your gift, you are free."

Her eyes burned with unshed tears as she set the shuttle down and stood.

"Werian?"

He had moved from the doorframe, coming closer, eyes wary. "Are you all right? What can I do?"

"You can sail me around the world, my fae prince."

"Truly? But I thought—"

She silenced him with a kiss. "Anyone can read the loom now. I am free to adventure with you. Just like we planned."

"Like we planned on our very first meeting."

"Exactly so."

He shouted and whirled her around while her imagination sewed the pattern of happily ever after across her heart.

READERS,

I hope you had as much fun reading this story as I did writing it. Please consider reviewing this book. Reviews make or break a book series, so the power is in your hands! :)

https://www.amazon.com/review/create-review?
asin=B08RSWGZXW

Up next is Wylfen princess Brielle and Balaur prince Dorin's story!

For exclusive bonus material from this series including a bonus scene, new maps, and exclusive character art, sign up for my newsletter, Alisha's Fantasy Fans.

https://www.alishaklapheke.com/free-prequel-1

Thanks and I hope you have an enchanting day! ;)

Alisha

SNEAK PEEK OF THE EDINBURGH SEER, ANOTHER FANTASY ROMANCE BY ALISHA KLAPHEKE

*SET IN AN ALTERNATE VERSION OF THE MODERN WORLD WITH A FEISTY SEER AND A HOT SCOT

The morning sun had just managed to paint a pale yellow light over Edinburgh's Old Town, and, as usual, Aini MacGregor had already run three errands and set up her father's candy lab for the day's work. Pots, scrubbed and warmed, on the stove. Measuring spoons shined to make the morning sun jealous. Bags of powdered sugar and vials of hormones and chemicals standing in place like disciplined kingsmen. Everything was exactly where it needed to be.

The tower was chilly this time of day and goosebumps hurried over Aini's skin as she unscrewed a jar and shifted the newly purchased cinnamon into its tidy home. She inhaled the lovely scent. Tears burned her eyes—not because of the many spices she had at her fingertips, but because of the rasping voice carried on the wind through the cracked, leaded window above her head—the voice of Nathair Campbell, the very powerful man who would shoot her dead if he knew what she was.

A sixth-senser.

Demanding her skittering heart to quit distracting her, Aini continued about her work. Today would be a great one for her father, Lewis MacGregor, crafter of the nobility's beloved sweets. Together, with the apprentices' help, they shaped goodies that not only tasted divine, but gave the eater certain short-term abilities usually enjoyed by birds or insects, or only dreamed up by wild imaginations. They'd been a hit at the king's last birthday party. The British king was a terrible man—Aini couldn't change that—but at least his parties helped with business. With the vision-inducing gum they were about to craft and test, the MacGregor business, Enliven, was poised to rule the boutique sweets market. If only the stupid thugs, the Campbells, would leave well enough alone.

Clan Campbell worked for the king, maintaining his rules here in Scotland. But lately...they seemed to have become very full of themselves and were taking on projects that Aini was certain the king himself knew nothing about.

"Who is shouting to wake the dead in the Grassmarket?" Neve demanded in place of a *Good Morning*. Father's female apprentice padded into the room. When she wasn't working in the lab, Neve took tourists around Scotland with Caledonia Tours. She knew her history, that was for sure.

With quick fingers and a smile, the Edinburgh native pulled her hair into two high buns and secured them with pins. All the girls here wore their hair like that. Aini tugged at one of her own heavy, black locks. It refused to be tied up, but even though it made her stand out—not many half Balinese girls in Scotland—she couldn't hate it. It reminded her of her mom, a woman who hadn't been perfect, but who'd loved her completely.

Aini straightened her lab coat and eyed the king's rules hanging on the wall. An identical list of "Scottish citizens cannot do this" and "All citizens and colonials must do that" were posted in every pub, home, and store in the entire British Empire. Even across the pond in the rebellious Dominion of New England colonies. Aini wondered if they'd ever get over their 18th century loss. They were nearly as bad as the Scottish rebels here.

Blinking, she remembered Neve's earlier question. "Nathair Campbell is down there, dirtying the morning."

Neve made a Scottish sound of disgust in the back of her throat. Aini couldn't have agreed more. "I'm excited about that new gum recipe," Neve said.

Perfectly on time—because Aini perfectly timed it— the gum base started to bubble on the stove.

"Your white pepper idea for the gum is going to work. I can feel it." Aini wiped her hands on a towel, breathing in the sweet smells. "I really think it'll trigger the chewer's schema for fire."

Neve grinned, and Aini realized her Dominion of New England accent was blazing again.

Thane loped into the lab, and Aini's heart whirred like a broken taffy puller and pushed every other thought out of her head. At six-foot-four, the Scotsman dominated the room, all broad shoulders, gray flashing eyes, and downturned mouth. He pulled his glasses out of his messy, honey-colored hair and headed toward his lab coat on the far hook. Mud caked the toes of his boots, and a silver necklace winked from his collarbone.

Because of who Aini was, and *what* Aini was, Thane with his late nights and penchant for whisky was the very definition of *Look, but don't touch*. She had to be careful. Do nothing dangerous. Never break any rules.

"Good morning, Thane."

Just because he wasn't for her didn't mean she had to be rude. After all, he was Father's favorite, besides herself, of course. Thane had developed the original formula for the vision gum. Aini wished she had half the brains he did.

"We're almost ready to mix," she said.

His gaze slid over her fingers and up her arms, and he gave her a nod.

As Neve measured out the pepper, Aini held a hand toward the bubbling broiler. "A little help?" she asked Thane. Her face heated. Why did her cheeks have to flush so easily?

"Aye. Course." Thane's thick, West Scots accent wrapped around every O and tripped over each R beautifully.

Tugging his coat on, Thane slid his glasses onto his slightly overlarge nose. Tattoos of chemical formulas snaked down his fingers in black letters, tiny numbers, and mathematical symbols. Aini leaned forward a little. $NaCl$ was salt. Another finger had a V over a t and—*oh*—it was the formula for viscosity. But the other markings? She could never quite get a good look at them.

Father walked in, wearing his usual style—all black under his lab coat, and every item ironed into full submission. He winked before readying the powdered sugar at the lab's silver table. He still wore his wedding ring, though the divorce happened long before Aini's mother died two years ago. She sighed, wishing she could do something about that pain.

"I was thinking," Father said to Thane, "if we used a pressure cooker to force the Maillard reaction in tomorrow's Dulce de Leche recipe..."

Thane's face brightened. "We could decrease the cooking time by perhaps six times." Thane lifted the pot as Aini stirred. His arm brushed hers and she swallowed. "Genius, Mr. MacGregor," Thane said.

"Will you never stop with the Mr. MacGregor? Just Lewis, please."

Thane smiled at Father like he was his own, like Father could somehow heal the hurt that clouded the uni student's eyes. But it was all right. She wasn't jealous. Aini knew Father was good at providing a stable life, a simple and scheduled way of living, something maybe Thane hadn't experienced before apprenticing here.

"Neve, will you please warm up the mixer?" Father wiped a spot of sugar off his nose and set his planner on the desk near the far end of the lab. The green and blue sugar, in the jars he'd mounted on the whitewashed wall, sparkled. He frowned like there was something unpleasant about them. Aini touched her chin. She'd always wondered why he displayed the jars like that. They'd never used those colored sugars and surely it would be better to have them with the other ingredients, organized by the lab table. She'd look into it later.

Father shook his head and went to help Thane pour the steaming gum base into the powdered sugar.

The lab's landline rang and Aini picked up. A familiar,

rough voice asked for Lewis MacGregor. Aini gritted her teeth. Not *them* again. Her grip on the phone tightened.

"Hold please." She looked to Father. "It's for you."

He stared at the ceiling, eyes pressed closed, before finally taking the call.

While Neve dealt with the mixer's perpetually moody switch across the room—all while humming a song loved by Father's other male apprentice, Myles—Aini took Father's place beside Thane.

Plunging her hands into the gum blend, she kneaded the sticky stuff. The mix was ready for flavor. The powdered sage, white pepper, and smoky nutmeg did nothing to improve the color of the chewing gum, but she was pretty sure Neve was on to something with this flavor choice. The herbs and spices, along with the medieval art packaging that Myles had drawn up, might just get people seeing ancient castles and feasts in great halls. Chemistry crossed with suggestion. It was how the human brain worked.

"No." Father's knuckles whitened as he squeezed the phone. "I'm not going to weaponize my products. Not until I see the royal approval. I'm finished talking about this." He punched a button and threw the phone to his desk where it banged against his laptop. "Campbells. Pushing and pushing. Playing both sides, and I know very well I'm not going to be the winner no matter how..." Muttering, he stalked back to the table. "I need to get something from my downstairs office. Give me a shout when we're ready to test." He disappeared down the staircase, growling about being left in peace.

The Campbells made up the majority of kingsmen stationed in Edinburgh. Normally, they were the law, acting as the king's agents, along with the other kingsmen. But since that public execution of those rebels last month, things had been different. Nathair Campbell had executed Scottish subjects without a trial of any kind. The king had excused him, blaming overzealous loyalty to the crown, but Aini wasn't so sure. Clan Campbell was less an arm of the king and more of a criminal gang these days. Aini couldn't believe they were pressuring Father to develop products that could covertly paralyze and poison without the king's seal of approval. Even if it was to fight the rebels. It was unfathomable.

Thane breathed hard through his nose like an angry horse.

She eyed the gum, looking for dry spots or uneven spicing. "What is it? What's off?"

Vine-like muscles twisted below Thane's rolled coat sleeves. He dusted his hands off and pushed his glasses into his hair. "If your father would agree to aid the Campbells, he'd be helping Scotland fight the rebels."

"He doesn't want to twist our craft into something sick and evil." She put her hands on her hips and powdered sugar puffed like little clouds. Flushing, she brushed herself off. "He's worked long and hard to establish Enliven. It's a boutique candy supplier. Not a government laboratory. Besides that, why can't the Campbells go through the official channels and find their own chemists if they're so set on this?"

Neve gathered the pre-blended gum mix. "Because Mr. MacGregor is the best chemist in the empire and they know it."

"Well, we're going to follow the official rules." Aini crossed her arms. "The king could shut us down and you know it."

Neve opened her mouth and closed it again. She hurried to the mixer and dropped her bundle into the metal bowl.

Aini chewed the inside of her cheek. She didn't want to be hard on Neve, but the rules were the rules.

"The Campbells and the king have the same goal, don't they?" Thane frowned. "What difference does fussing about with royal seals make?"

"If my father skirts the law like the Campbells want him to do, the Campbells might get away with it, but I seriously doubt he will."

An image flashed through her memory—an executed sixth-senser.

The woman had been about her mother's age. Aini remembered the lady's wispy, auburn hair. The black band across her eyes. Her body jerking as the bullet hit her chest. The red blood against her striped dress. Her clothing said native Edinburgh, the style Aini tried to imitate. But even fitting in hadn't saved her.

If Aini was found out, the Campbells would assume Father knew about her ability, which he didn't. She squeezed her hands together. She couldn't even think about him rotting in a dark cell.

When the gum was mixed and cooled, Thane cut the ropes into small pieces and Aini called her father back up to the lab. It was time to see if the gum really worked.

. . .

THE LIGHT THROUGH THE LAB'S WINDOWS CAST A NET OF gold around Aini's father as he peered at his watch. He handed Aini the clipboard of notes they'd destroy as soon as the trial was complete. They couldn't let anyone outside of Enliven get a hold of the information. The competition would leap at the chance to outdo them. Because of this, Aini and the rest had become very, very good at remembering recipes.

Neve and Aini found seats and Thane took a stool, ready to try the gum.

"Where is Myles anyway?" Neve asked.

Aini was actually glad Father's second male apprentice wasn't here. "Buying new paints for his adverts." Myles was great fun, but he could really be a distraction during tests like this.

Father stared at Thane. "I want to know the very minute—the exact moment—you see something." He started the timer on his watch.

"Aye," Thane popped the gum between his lips and chewed, rubbing a hand over his sharp chin.

"How's it taste, then?" Neve scooted forward on her stool.

"A bit fiery."

"Fiery?" Aini asked, pen poised over the clipboard. "Be more specific. We need details for the investors."

"Any visions yet?" Father inched closer to Thane.

Stumbling back, Thane's mouth dropped open, the gum on his tongue.

Aini laughed.

Father practically hopped on Thane. "What do you see, lad?" He normally hid his accent, wanting to please his many English clients, but excitement drew it right out of him.

Staring at the ceiling beams, Thane paled. "Translucent wings. About ten feet long. He's...he's..." The uni student ducked and laughed once, his Adam's apple bobbing in his throat. "He's breathing fire." He shoved his hands through his hair and knocked his glasses to the floor.

Neve hugged herself. "A dragon."

Father lifted his feet in a little jig and grabbed Aini's arm, pulling her into his dance. Heart light, she did a spin, then squeezed him, feeling safe and loved, as if everything was going to be okay.

"I can't believe it," Thane whispered.

Neve grinned. "I knew that white pepper would do the trick."

"Couldn't have done it without you, my wee squirrel," Father said to Aini. "The king will reward us handsomely, what with his birthday celebration coming up. We might get a tax exemption."

"And the elite will want it at their parties if the king has it at his," she said.

Father shouted, "Huzzah!" and zipped over to his desk to write something up.

Aini couldn't stop smiling. Another candy for their impressive inventory. Another building block for Father's beloved business. Somehow, she had to thank the apprentices for all their hard work. Maybe a special dinner or a big night out. This vision-inducing gum was another reason she loved having all of them here, a part of the family.

Neve peppered Thane with questions about the

formula. Over Neve's head, Thane met Aini's gaze. A shadow passed over his face. He was a melancholy sort, but this was more. Something...darker. Aini's smile faded. He had nothing to be upset about today. What could be bothering him? Surely not all this stuff about the Campbells. It would pass. Wouldn't it?

Father tugged Aini into another jubilant hug, and her smile returned. She could maintain this happiness. She would maintain it. No matter what. She just had to keep her sixth sense concealed. Because visions prompted by chewing gum earned money, but visions of another sort only led to death.

Buy/Download The Edinburgh Seer today!

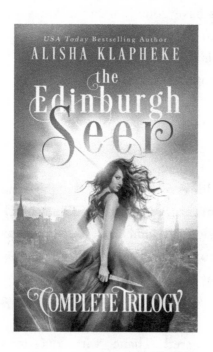